What people are say

Premonitio

Premonitions, the second book in the Recognitions series, opens with a prologue set in 1500s West Africa where a healer works his Premonitions magic on a baby and faces fear and gratitude from the villagers he helps. Fast-forward to 2018 New York City, where a mother faces her daughter's rising confidence and power and her own lasting changes as her confrontation with past lives lead her to separate from her husband after some twenty years of marriage. Amelia has confronted her husband's absence, his rush to a new life, and her own altered state of consciousness and life. Now she faces new consequences stemming from the publication of her book Recognitions and the results of decisions made in her altered life. By the third chapter, which takes place in France in 1776, it should be evident that Premonitions features a wandering timeline that reinforces past lives, experiences, and quests for love and family as it draws connections between people with ties that transcend time itself.

As readers probe each character's world, emotions, perceptions, and changes, they will delight in a story that evolves beyond the usual time slip or alternate lives exploration to probe the presence and impact of different kinds of magic in different cultures and eras. While Premonitions will best be ingested by those who enjoyed the background provided in Recognitions, it will also reach newcomers who look for novels of reincarnation, connections, and transformation. Uplifting and enlightening, Premonitions is a worthy sequel to Recognitions that deserves just as much acclaim as the first in the series.
Diane Donovan, *Midwest Book Review*

Premonitions grabs you from the first word, and keeps you hooked to the very last. So melodically written, with characters and timelines harmonising in perfect synchronicity, culminating in a story that piques our interest in human emotions and the depths of human experiences. A riveting read.

Reena Kumarasingham, author of *Shrouded Truth*

Daniela I. Norris captivates the reader with the way she weaves past-lives stories together and the sparkle of her narrative. A must read.

Andy Tomlinson, author of *Healing the Eternal Soul*

Premonitions by Daniela I. Norris is a book about three generations of people. Amelia has just ended a relationship with her daughter's fencing coach. Telling herself it is for the sake of the children, she is still trying to come to terms with the decision and undergoes hypnotherapy to help her with her anxieties. In sixteenth-century Africa, a shaman and his apprentice are witnesses to a horrific attack on their village when "ghost faced men" descend on their people and leave a trail of destruction. Spiriting away the young men of the village in chains, it is left to the apprentice to nurture the remaining villagers. Meanwhile, in the eighteenth century, Adele is the envy of her friends and family. She has an attentive husband, beautiful children, and a splendid house, but all is not well. Adele is wondering if the choice she made at eighteen was the right one or did her family pressure her into a marriage of convenience. What is it that links these three people? Is it a past life link or merely a coincidence?

I loved this book! In *Premonitions*, Daniela I. Norris whisks you through the centuries effortlessly. You are transported to the shaman's humble dwelling and feel the palpable fear of the villagers. The frustration of the French people who are starving on the streets of Paris while the aristocracy feast on banquets leaps from the page. This is a book that makes you wonder if past lives are an actual phenomenon or just the product of an active imagination. Whether you are a believer or not, this excellent book is a quality read and will keep you gripped until the final page.

Tracy Young, Readers' Favorite

Premonitions

Book II in the Recognitions Series

Premonitions

Book II in the Recognitions Series

Daniela I. Norris

Winchester, UK
Washington, USA

JOHN HUNT PUBLISHING

First published by Roundfire Books, 2019
Roundfire Books is an imprint of John Hunt Publishing Ltd., No. 3 East St., Alresford,
Hampshire SO24 9EE, UK
office@jhpbooks.net
www.johnhuntpublishing.com
www.roundfire-books.com

For distributor details and how to order please visit the 'Ordering' section on our website.

Text copyright: Daniela I. Norris 2018

ISBN: 978 1 78904 139 2
978 1 78904 140 8 (ebook)
Library of Congress Control Number: 2018948886

A CIP catalogue record for this book is available from the British Library.

Design: Stuart Davies

UK: Printed and bound by CPI Group (UK) Ltd, Croydon, CR0 4YY
US: Printed and bound by Thomson Shore, 7300 West Joy Road, Dexter, MI 48130

We operate a distinctive and ethical publishing philosophy in
all areas of our business, from our global network of authors to
production and worldwide distribution.

"Man is least himself when he talks in his own person. Give him a mask, and he will tell you the truth."
—Oscar Wilde

For all fencers — to their masks and to their truths

Prologue

West Africa, 1577

He lived on the outskirts. He did not like to go into the village but could see it from his hut; it often looked to him like some sort of an illusion – partly real, partly imaginary. The people walking about, tending to their daily chores, were like little floating dots, hovering randomly, unaware of the bigger picture. They only came to him when they needed something: a cure or a blessing. On rare and special occasions, someone asked for a curse.

He did not like to perform the latter. Delivering a curse felt like it went against the very grain of his being, against his natural ways. Yet, he did it every now and then, when he believed it might be justified.

His only company when clients did not come to see him was his ancestors. Their presence was always comforting and pleasant to him – they were not frightening, or stubborn, or ridiculous like some humans were. They were never mean or short-tempered. He felt more comfortable in their presence than in that of the village people, or of those who walked for entire days, or rowed for hours down the river, just to come and see him. He was a well-known healer and sorcerer in this area – admired and feared by many.

There was one thing he never felt and was not sure he would in his lifetime, and that was absolutely fine with him. He never felt loved.

Now there is a woman approaching, a baby tied to her back. She emerges in front of his eyes as if coming out from a cloud of mist. Is she real? Is she not? He decides she is real the moment he notices that in her hands she carries something wrapped in cloth, maybe an offering to him. As she gets nearer he can see the details – her ashen face and sunken eyes.

"My child," he says. She is a child indeed, her skin fresh despite the sadness in her eyes and the smell she brings is that of cooking-fire and fragrant herbs. "What can I help you with?"

She utters a guttural sound, like a wounded animal, as her fingers start undoing the knot on the fabric tied beneath her bosom. She lets the two parts of the fabric slip and he catches the small child behind her back, holding onto its scrawny bottom.

He takes the infant in his arms and sits cross-legged. He then closes his eyes and starts humming. The sound comes from the pit of his stomach and his body rocks backward and forward to a melody that he can hear in his mind. A stream of words that has no meaning to the young mother standing in front of him slips through his lips, giving his face a grim appearance as he starts talking in tongues. The sounds coming out of his mouth make no sense to him, or to the mother, but they do seem to make sense to some small creatures gathering around him and watching with curiosity. A lizard, a few birds, a small monkey with beady black eyes peeking out of the branches where it feels safe enough to hide and try to aim a nut or two at the young woman sitting underneath.

This goes on for some time, and the mother watches him while he rocks her infant son in his arms. At first, she breathes heavily, her mind filled with worry. But then, as the chanting goes on she appears to be giving in to a sensation that envelops her like a cool breeze; to a knowing that descends on her when she looks at the healer's calm face.

"Here you go," he says after what seems like forever, but in reality is no more than a small fraction of time passing. He hands her the child, whose small chest now visibly rises with every breath.

The healer gets up and goes into his hut, emerging a few moments later with two animal-skin bags. He dips his middle finger into the smaller sachet and when he takes it out, it is covered in thin, white powder. He marks three horizontal lines on the child's forehead.

"For protection," he tells the young mother. She nods.

He then puts his hand into the larger bag and takes out a fist full of herbs. He rolls the herbs in a small cloth and gives the young woman exact instructions as to how to prepare them for the boy. She nods silently.

"Come back to me after three moons," he says.

She nods again, silently putting a small offering at his feet. She then swings the child onto her back and fastens the long piece of fabric under her bosom again. She takes a few steps backwards, as if not wanting to turn her back to the healer. He can feel her apprehension, mixed with gratitude. He is used to this; he has become familiar with the vibrations he senses – whenever he does an act of healing for someone, how they are grateful, but fearful. Fearful of him and of his powers. Yet he knows these powers are not his own; they are only borrowed powers. These are merely powers that he has access to but that are also harmful if not used correctly. Every time he calls on his forefathers and on his spirit guides for help, he imagines himself as a hollow branch, a tube through which these powers flow – through him and onto the person who needs healing. And when he calls they always come, his forefathers and his spirit guides, offering advice and healing.

He is deep in his thoughts when he notices that the woman is still there, looking at him from a short distance away.

He stares at her when he suddenly feels something he can only think of as tenderness flow from her to him. This is something he is not used to. Respect? Yes. Fear? Of course. But tenderness is a feeling he had not experienced very often. It makes him uncomfortable. And there is something else, not tangible, nothing he can put his fingers on, but he just knows that this feeling of *deja vu* is because this has already happened before.

Maybe in one of my dreams, he thinks. Having premonitions and feelings of *deja vu* are not a rare occurrence for him, that much he knows. In fact, they feel like second nature, but at the same time are still a bit eerie every time they happen.

The woman keeps looking at him, seeming reluctant to leave. Maybe she doesn't understand him?

He raises three fingers at her.

"In three moons," he repeats. "Now you must go."

And she does; she turns around and walks away carrying the sleeping infant on her back as if it was a rag-doll.

Three moons later she returns. He can hear her before he sees her, the child on her back squealing in delight. It is late afternoon and the sun is beginning its descent behind the trees. The leaves rustle as small animals and large birds make their presence known to him in a cacophony of screeches and songs. He is never a threat to them. His sustenance always comes from gifts people bring. He has no need to hunt. On his daily expeditions to the nearby forest, he gathers medicinal plants and roots – some of the roots he boils and eats. He knows them well by now, can tell the ones that give him strange dreams from the ones that fill his stomach and sometimes make him feel bloated. Every once in a while he gets an offering of meat – usually antelope or gnu meat. Someone once brought meat from a monkey, which he did not eat. However, he did use it for one of his rituals.

As the woman draws closer, he can see the child sitting upright on her back, holding onto his mother's shoulders, his little feet kicking the air.

He greets them with a nod and sees the woman smiling at him. Her smile conveys joy, and something else – something he cannot quite understand. He is much better at interpreting energies than sensing real human emotions. There is nothing more to be said, as the child is obviously well. But it is she who has something for him. It is some kind of fragrant stew, made in gratitude for healing her son.

She sets it in front of him and says something. Or at least he thinks she does, as her lips move, but only an animal-like sound comes out. And then he realizes what is strange about her. She is deaf-mute.

He looks at her and then down at the small wooden bowl in front of him. Saliva fills his mouth and he realizes he has not eaten something that smelled so good in a long time. As if reading his mind, the woman nods and takes a few steps back. She motions with her hand to her mouth, telling him to eat.

She then leaves him to eat his meal, and as she walks away he can make out among the squeals of the monkeys and the singing of the birds the babbling of the young child.

The child can't be deaf, or he would not be making these sounds, he thinks. *But the mother cannot hear her own child's voice.*

He eats a mouthful of deliciously cooked roots and herbs and an unfamiliar joy fills him like water filling the nearby river after the rainy season – it feels plentiful and clear and powerful.

ONE

New York, 2018

It was not where I thought I'd find myself on my forty-fifth birthday. I imagined I'd be sitting on some tropical beach with a cold drink in my hand, maybe with a pink umbrella to complete the cliché. Perhaps gazing at a crystal-clear sea, with Don sitting next to me. But that's not how life turned out.

As it happened, I almost forgot it was my birthday, as I sat on the bleachers in a large sports center, watching a fencing competition.

It was nearly the end of the bout and I was trying to stop myself from biting my nails. I certainly wasn't going to shout random things in Jen's direction, like some of the other parents did, embarrassing their kids in the process. What did I know about fencing, anyway? I only knew that it changed my daughter's life. That from an awkward preteen she turned into a confident, kick-ass teenage girl wielding a sword with such confidence, as if she'd been doing it since the day she was born. It helped that she was a left-hander, just like Noah, her coach.

"This is actually a slight advantage, Mom," she explained to me a week ago. "Noah says that because there are not as many left-handed fencers, when I fence a right-handed person, they can often be caught off-guard. It's because they are not as used to fencing someone left-handed, the hits are kind of different. But you know what?" she asked with a wide smile.

"What?" I had to ask.

"I discovered that I can actually fence with both hands!" she said triumphantly, as if she'd just announced that she discovered a new planet.

That was Jen, always living life to the fullest. I knew that if she continued like that, she was highly likely to get where she wanted in life—wherever that may be.

Now Jen was in the lead with 13 touches—the other fencer had only 11, but the bout was far from over. She still had two points to go if she were to win, and those two points were far from certain. Her opponent was a thin, tall brunette, an excellent fencer. Her coach yelled instructions at her, which she surely could not hear under the fencing mask, in the heat of the bout. The coach wasn't even supposed to be talking to her during the match—only during the breaks, but the referee did not call him out on it.

On Jen's side of the strip Noah stood silently, brooding, his fists clenched. He was not the yelling type. I watched him bite his nails at the end of the strip, his face dark and serious.

I tried to push our last conversation to the back of my mind and focus on the bout. I knew he was doing his best to help Jen win, despite the fact her mother had just dumped him a couple of weeks before.

Well, I didn't really dump him as such—how could I? My heart ached for him, or because of him, I wasn't sure which one was more accurate. Even my body ached for his touch. But somehow, I still don't know exactly how it happened, Don made me feel obliged—for the sake of the children if nothing else—to give him another chance.

Don just freaked out on me when I came to get Tom and Jen from his place after my solo trip to France, over a month ago. I went to Paris for some work meetings with French publishers who were considering purchasing the translation rights to some of the books we were about to publish. Then I continued to the Pays de Gex, near Geneva, a place I'd never even heard of a few months back. The Pays de Gex was the backdrop of some strange visions I had—for lack of a better description. That was where I've seen something, several things, that could have perhaps been glimpses of past lives, or maybe they were just my overactive imagination. One way or another, these were experiences I had during hypnotherapy sessions following my personal difficulties, insomnia, and anxieties—all a result of my separation from Don after twenty years of marriage.

But Don didn't see it like that; he wouldn't understand even if I found the words and the courage to tell him that I went to see a hypnotherapist. And not only that I went to see a hypnotherapist—I also had experiences and dreams I could not explain. It started with visions of a French girl living in a small village at the foothills of the Jura Mountains in the eighteenth century. It continued with visions of an African medicine man trying to save the young men in his village from a destiny of slavery, sometime around the fifteenth century.

I had visions and dreams I could not completely understand; I could not explain them to myself, certainly not to Don. Don knew me as a down-to-earth person, not as someone who believed in past lives, spiritual visioning, dreams that had meaning or any of that kind of stuff.

Then he completely lost it.

"Who did you go with?" he asked in a harsh voice that very quickly turned sheepish when I stared at him disbelievingly.

"That's not really your business anymore," I said. "You've got Claudette, remember?"

He'd been shacked up with skinny Claudette for nearly a year now, ever since we separated.

"She is not the reason for our separation," he said, and I was shocked to notice tears in his eyes as he sat across from me in a small restaurant in the Village a couple of days later. I could not recall when I ever saw tears in his eyes—maybe right after the birth of our first baby, Tom—but that was over sixteen years ago now. And if he had had tears in his eyes on other occasions in the past, they certainly had nothing to do with me, or with our separation.

"We decided to separate for other reasons," he sniffled.

"But we said we'd just try it out," I reminded him. "We said we just needed some space from each other, to see how it feels. What was the rush to move in with Claudette?"

He looked at me with puppy eyes.

"I don't know," he said. "I guess it was a mistake."

My throat suddenly felt dry. I took a small sip from my wineglass.

"A big one," I said.

"I know."

There was a long pause.

"Think about the kids," he said. "We owe it to them to try again."

Emotional blackmail was never a thing he'd done well, I thought.

"That's not fair," I said. "You didn't think about Tom and Jen when you started a new life, did you? They're kind of used to it now. And so am I."

He leaned forward across the table and took my hand in his.

"Amelia, I know I messed up. I really do. Will you please let me try and fix it?"

I don't know why, I have really no idea why, but I said, "Maybe."

And then, a couple of days later, I called Noah.

"We need to talk," I said. But he knew. Somehow, he already knew.

"Do you want to meet up or do you just want to say it on the phone?" he asked in that mechanical voice he had when he didn't quite know how he was supposed to react to something.

"Don asked me to give him another chance," I said.

He didn't say anything, but I could sense him holding his breath on the other end of the line.

"I am sorry," I said. "So sorry, but we kind of owe it to Jen and Tom to try. At least to try."

Noah still didn't speak.

"Say something," I begged. "Anything."

I felt a dull pain in the pit of my stomach, and then—not sure why—a small hope. A small hope that Noah would try to object, disagree, convince, argue. That he'd say, *Don't go back to Don. Stay with me. We can make it work.*

But he didn't say any of that.

"I hope you'll be happy," was all he said.

"Thank you," I said.

I put the phone down and wiped the tears off my cheeks.

Then I reached for a copy of my novel, *Recognitions*, its first draft now completed. Writing this novel had changed my life; changed the way I looked at most things.

Leafing through the pages with shaking fingers, I opened the manuscript on a random page, around a third of the way in. It was page 73.

My eyes stopped on the one-before-last paragraph. As the letters floated before me, I felt tears welling up again.

"Your schoolteacher does like you, he has come by recently several times, hasn't he? No man does that if he has no interest," said Madame Durand. "But he is timid and he does not speak his mind. I am not sure if this is a positive quality in a man, for he will lose many good things in life because of this character trait. Men who achieve things have to reach out and take them, have to be able to fight for them."

So, I thought to myself, *perhaps he hasn't learned that yet.*

TWO

Gex, France, 1776

Adele saw the schoolteacher in town once in a while, but never dared speak to him directly. She was rarely alone, and in any case the look he gave her—even from across the street—almost made her cry. In fact it did make her cry, but she managed to restrain herself until later and cry at home, when she had finished all of the day's duties and found a quiet corner to sit and reflect on her life choices. The life choices that did not seem real, did not even seem to be her own, but she knew that they were. After all, she had made them, hadn't she? It was foolish to blame her parents, or her friends, or anyone else who encouraged her to marry for status and for money.

Nonetheless, she felt robbed of the chance of living the kind of life she really wanted to live: a life of adventure, of travel, of doing something that mattered, of experiencing real love.

"Is everything all right?" asked Pierre one evening, and she just nodded. Everything wasn't all right; she had seen the schoolteacher in town that morning and did not dare speak to him. He looked sad to see her, sad but proud. He was not a man to complain, he was not one to seek revenge for hurt pride, and she knew that much. But she so wanted to cross the street, take his hand, tell him she was sorry.

She was indeed sorry—sorry for failing him, sorry for making her choice for the wrong reason, sorry she could not love him like he deserved to be loved. But, of course, she could not say that—not to him, certainly not to her husband Pierre, not even to herself.

She had two small children now, and they kept her busy.

There was also the house to look after—even with two maids, there was much to do. And so, she put on a brave face and tried to get on with life.

Their house was bigger than her parents' home and was not far from the Bertrand family residence, in the center of Gex. There was a girl who did the cleaning and most of the cooking, and a nanny who came to help with the children every morning. This was more than Adele's mother ever had. But Pierre would not let Adele come and work at the store despite her frequent requests.

"It would be nice to see some people now and then," she said.

"You see people all the time," he said. "You see the children, and you see my mother, and your parents, don't you? I can take care of the store."

She had the distinct impression that he was trying to keep her from the world, tucked away in their comfortable home, which now often felt more like a prison. All her dreams of ballroom dances in Paris and adventures in London seemed more unattainable than ever. Pierre had not mentioned taking her to Paris since the day they were married, some six years back.

They had a carriage and a coachman—Pierre would not be seen walking around town like a peasant and never cared much for sitting on horseback himself—so she took the children to her parents' house every other day. There, she would sit with her mother and work on her embroidery for an hour or two—the same kind of embroidery she used to hate so much—while the children played in the garden.

"You seem so domesticated," said Anne Durand. "Aren't you happy to have some home help, now that you see what it is like to raise two children?"

"I feel like my life is over," said Adele.

Her mother stuck her needle in her own embroidery and raised her eyes to meet Adele's.

"Don't say that," she said. "That sounds ungrateful."

"Well, maybe I am ungrateful," said Adele.

Anne Durand sighed.

They both continued their work in silence, until the children ran in, demanding lunch.

"I am so hungry, *maman*," said Delphine. She was nearly four now, and expressed herself well. Her little brother, Yves, was only two and a half. Two children in four years was a demanding task, on Adele's body, and on her soul. She didn't move from her chair despite the little girl whining and pulling on her arm.

"Come, come," said Madame Durand.

She took the children to the kitchen and gave them lunch, leaving Adele to stare at her embroidery as if it would come to life or transform into a genie who'd grant her three wishes, if she looked at it long enough.

Adele could not say what was wrong, but she woke in the mornings with a heavy heart. Some mornings she did not even feel like getting out of bed. The truth was, she felt that the life she really wanted to live was different, but in what way she could, or would not, quite say. It had escaped her: both the meaning of her life, and life itself.

"She needs fresh air," said the doctor Pierre had called some weeks before. "She needs distraction, perhaps some more help with the children."

And so Pierre asked his own mother to take the children to her house more often, after the nanny who looked after them had left in the afternoons.

Adele could not really complain that the children were a burden on her. They were not—they were clever, perky children who liked to run around and explore. She just didn't have the energy to explore with them.

All she wanted to do most days was to stay in bed and read a book. But she could not be seen by the home help reading all morning, for those horrible women—who couldn't read them-

selves and saw it as a waste of time—would surely gossip about
the lazy young Madame Bertrand, and that gossip would reach
her mother-in-law who seemed constantly to be looking for faults
in Adele's character. The older Madame Bertrand may even try
to use Adele's reading of useless novels as proof that she, Adele,
needed to be committed to some institution where they knew
how to deal with women who did not know their place in the
world. Adele thought she'd heard it whispered, some months
back, when the older Madame Bertrand did not know Adele was
not far from her, having just come in from the garden to fetch
some gloves for Delphine.

"It's not easy to raise children," her own mother told her
more than once. "But at least you are married to a man who can
provide well for you and the children..."

"Pierre doesn't care about the children and about me as much
as he cares about his precious business," said Adele, not looking
her mother in the eye.

Was it as obvious to her mother, as it was obvious to her that
she was the one constantly looking for faults in her husband's
character?

After all, her mother was right. Pierre was a good husband
who provided well for her and their children. But it seemed
that after the wedding and the birth of Delphine and then Yves,
Pierre's enthusiasm for her had somewhat diminished. And he
certainly forgot the promises he'd made to her before they were
married. He thought Adele should be happy simply because she
was married to him; that should be enough to keep any woman
happy in his view, especially the daughter of a *paysan*.

"Perhaps you can try and do more to maintain his interest,"
suggested her friend Eugénie, when Adele dared mention these
thoughts to her. But what did Eugénie know? She was now married to one of the local farmers, and they did not have children
despite wanting them. It just didn't happen for them.

However, Eugénie was very much in love with her farmer

Emil, who was a handsome and strong young man even if he was barely literate. It didn't seem to matter to Eugénie, who followed her husband around like a domesticated duck and doted on him when he came back from the fields in the late afternoons.

"You are so fortunate," said Eugénie more than once. "You married so well."

But Adele could not help but wonder ... *what if?*

What if she hadn't listened to her mother, and had married Jules Badeau, the schoolteacher, instead of marrying Pierre Bertrand, the well-off merchant's son?

Rumors said that the schoolteacher, the same kind and gentle man that her mother claimed would not be able to provide her—Adele—with a comfortable life, was spending his time in important circles these days. He was now a regular guest at Voltaire's chateau in Ferney, and was even seen in Geneva once or twice together with Monsieur Voltaire!

"Monsieur Voltaire even sends his carriage for him," whispered their neighbor, Madame Montagne, during one of her afternoon visits when Adele sat staring at her embroidery, imagining she was somewhere else instead. "Monsieur Voltaire does not like his guests to have to walk all the way from Gex," added Madame Montagne knowingly, as if walking was a bad thing.

She and Pierre would get along just fine together, thought Adele, not without bitterness. She was confident that Jules Badeau, unless he changed significantly over the past six years, did not at all mind walking.

It did not help the situation that the schoolteacher did not marry. He seemed more distant and more distracted than ever on the times he crossed paths with Adele on the streets of Gex. They nodded to each other like two distant acquaintances. But her heart ached for weeks after each such encounter, and she could not help but wonder if his did, too.

Why doesn't he marry one of the local girls? She kept wondering.

Then, after not having seen him for several months, she heard a rumor that he had moved back to the city of Lyon. Madame Montagne visited Adele's mother while she was there with the children, and mentioned it in passing.

"The schoolteacher from Gex, who came from Lyon, remember him? The one who was so fond of Adele. He moved back to Lyon, apparently to do some professional training," she said to Anne Durand. Adele pretended not to listen, but she drank in every word.

"What kind of training?" asked Madame Durand, glancing sideways at her daughter.

"Someone told me that he is training as a *maître d'armes*, a fencing master," said Madame Montagne. "And you know who sent him there? Monsieur Voltaire, of course. Apparently the two men share a passion for fencing and now Monsieur Badeau is making a profession of it, it seems, with Monsieur Voltaire's encouragement and funding. When he finishes his training as a *maître d'armes* he will be teaching young boys to fence as well as to read and write," she added knowingly.

"Not a very practical skill in our parts," said Anne Durand. "But of course, perhaps in Lyon it is...and of course, he could always find work in Paris."

"That is not what I've heard," whispered Madame Montagne. "I heard that Monsieur Voltaire insists on this: he wants to bring fencing to our land as a necessary skill for young boys, so they can defend themselves in duels against the arrogant young men from Paris and Lyon. Monsieur Voltaire himself was a victim, in his youth, to such arrogance. He even had to leave France and live in England for some time as a result of an encounter that ended badly. Imagine that! Having to move to *Angleterre*."

"Living in England, *pfff*," said Anne Durand.

Adele, who was standing by the table, steadied herself by leaning on it.

"Are you all right, my dear?" asked Madame Montagne.

"Yes, of course," said Adele. "My head was just spinning a

little."

"You had better sit down then," said Madame Montagne and pulled out the chair next to her. "You are not with child again, dear, are you?" she added, smiling a conspirator's smile. "They are so much work at this age, the little ones," she said to Anne Durand, Adele's mother. "But your daughter is lucky, she married well. She has so much home help, does she not?"

"I am sorry, I feel nauseous. I need some fresh air," whispered Adele and rushed outside.

Madame Montagne rubbed her hands together and smiled, looking very pleased with herself. Now she would have something to tell Madame Mercier, whom she was scheduled to visit later that afternoon.

Anne Durand sighed and followed her daughter outside.

Adele has been distracted over the past week—she could not remember where she had put things down, she burned the *tarte* she baked after collecting apples from the tree in their garden and she had forgotten to take the children to her mother-in-law at the designated time the day before. They played outside and she just sat there and stared at them, until she remembered that Madame Bertrand was expecting them and she rushed over to the Bertrand residence, arriving with the children but without their coats, all wild-haired and confused.

The next day was a Sunday, and they went to church in town, for Madame Bertrand insisted that Pierre and Adele come with the children. Pierre, as always, obliged.

They took the carriage despite the short distance from their home to church, and Pierre insisted that the coach drop them off right in front of the entrance. They walked in and found Monsieur and Madame Bertrand, and sat next to them in the third row. And he, the schoolteacher, was there, sitting just a few rows behind them.

What was Jules doing there, in church, on a Sunday morning? She wondered. He'd voiced his real opinions about religion to her privately on one of their long walks together in the year before she was married to Pierre.

"Religion keeps people where those who control them want them to stay," was what he said to her back then. *But perhaps he had to keep up appearances.*

She dared not turn and look at him directly, but she felt his eyes burning a hole in her back, a hole that went all the way into her heart.

The service was a blur and the children were a welcome distraction—she had to hush them every few moments. She wore her Sunday best—but these days she had many dresses to choose from; it was very different from just some years back, before she married Pierre Bertrand and only had one good Sunday dress.

On the way out, they walked past him—and he, Jules Badeau, sat there, frozen on the pew. Pierre tipped his hat at him. Jules nodded, and it was only later she realized that neither of them dared look each other in the eye.

"What's the matter, Adele?" asked Pierre one evening, as she sat in front of the fire, staring at the flames, while he worked on the store's accounting books.

Adele did not hear the question, and Pierre had to repeat it.

"Adele?" he touched her shoulder, and she looked at him, startled.

"Is everything all right?" he asked.

"Yes, of course…" she said. "I am just a little tired."

"You've been tired a lot recently," he said.

Adele just shook her head.

"I suppose it's the children…"

The children had been in bed for a while now, and Adele tried to work up the energy to go into the bedroom she shared with Pierre, change into her nightdress and collapse in bed for another night in which sleep would surely escape her.

She was sleepy during the day but wide-awake at night, lying in bed next to Pierre, listening to his rhythmic breathing.

Why am I so dissatisfied with my life, she kept wondering, and could not come up with an answer.

She had a good husband, two wonderful children, a nice home.

But in those few nights when she would get some sleep, she'd sometimes wake up remembering the ghost of a dream.

In the pre-dawn hours, she could almost grasp the remainder of the feeling of what it was like to dance in a ballroom in Paris, her fine blue silk dress twirling around her in gentle waves. And when she tried to get a glimpse of her dancing partner, she could never actually see him—but she had a feeling, a strong feeling that left little room for doubt. Through the eyes of sleep and the chirruping of the early-rising birds, she knew without a doubt that the dance partner in her dream was the schoolteacher.

THREE

New York, 2018

I could hardly believe how much Jen had changed over the past months. From a quiet and shy girl, she'd become this confident, radiant young woman—transformed almost overnight. Was it the teenage hormones doing their thing?

"No, Mom," she said, between two bites of her veggie burger. "It's the fencing. It really changed my life. It's as if I found what I've always wanted to do."

This was a pretty deep observation coming from a nearly fifteen-year-old, and I told her so.

"Well," she said, "I guess I am growing up."

She was indeed growing up, and it scared me. I didn't mention Gabriel—the boy who sparked her initial interest in fencing nearly a year ago. It seemed as if she'd forgotten all about him in her newfound passion for the sport. Maybe he was just the vehicle to get her into the world of fencing, who knows.

But there was something else—something that worried me slightly. It was her relationship with her coach, Noah. It seemed to be different and separate from my relationship with him; there was a loyalty that I've never seen before in Jen, as if she's taken on some kind of apprenticeship with him. He seemed to have become her mentor, to be consulted on more than just fencing-related topics. Topics she should have been discussing with her father, or me, for example.

I took her out for dinner after her training on a Tuesday evening. We picked a small restaurant not far from Times Square. The early evening rain had just stopped, coloring everything in a bright pallet of freshness. I wasn't sure how to bring up the topic that I've been struggling with for the past couple of weeks.

"How do you feel about your dad and I getting back together?" I finally asked.

She chewed a bite, carefully considering her answer.

"I don't know," she said. "You don't seem happy together."

Bam. Straight to the heart of the matter.

Don hasn't officially moved back in with us, but he did spend most evenings at our place. We ate dinner together a few times a week, and he acted as if nothing had happened—as if he hasn't been absent from our lives in the past year. He claimed his place with a typical Don self-confidence, as if he deserved to be let back into our lives, as if there wasn't even a question about it. I managed to keep him out of my bedroom, and in the few nights he did stay over, he slept on the couch.

"Did you get back together for our sake, Mom? Because if you did, that's not right," Jen said. She now stopped eating and was searching for my eyes.

"Tom seems happy to have his dad around," I said. And I knew that was undoubtedly true, because Tom missed his dad. Now sixteen, he needed a male role model, and even though I wasn't convinced I wanted him to turn out like Don, I realized the importance of having his father around.

But Jen…it was as if she had no interest in her father. She seemed to have adopted Noah as an alternative father figure, which I did find somewhat disturbing.

"So did you train with Sergey today?" I asked, but immediately realized I was not off the hook.

"You're changing the subject, Mom," said Jen. "Did you get back with Dad for us, or for you?"

I decided to try the truth. I felt as if I could talk to her about almost anything now—anything, except the one topic I was trying to avoid, of course.

"I don't know," I said. "I suppose it's a little of both."

"And what about Noah?"

I didn't expect her to be so direct.

"What about him?"

"Oh, Mom. Come on, you know what I am talking about."

"Why don't you tell me, because I am not sure I do."

"He likes you so much, Mom. He more than likes you, he is...
He seems so sad since you went back to Dad. And Dad...he had
this other woman, he only wants you now because you're in love
with someone else."

I looked at her, uncertain how to reply to this, but I suspect
that my eyes said everything there was to say.

"Whose side you on, anyway?" I asked.

"Actually, I am on your side, Mom. And a little bit on Noah's."

"Why is that?"

She paused, thinking about what to say next.

"I can't explain it really. It just feels as if...as if you're meant
to be together."

Before I could think of an appropriate answer, my cell phone
rang. I had a glance at the screen—it was Don.

"Hi, Don," I said.

"Are you coming home?" he asked.

"Jen and I are having dinner together. We'll be home in an
hour, maybe a bit more."

"Oh," he said. "I forgot. I guess I'll order a pizza for Tom and
me. He got back from school hungry."

"Yes," I said. "He usually does."

"So you're with Jen?" he asked.

"I just told you," I said. "And I also told you this morning."

"Right," he said. "See you later, then."

"Later."

I hung up.

"You look upset, what did he say?" asked Jen.

"Oh, nothing, just wanted to know where we were."

"But you told him this morning."

"Yes, Jen, I did."

What I didn't say was that Don must have gotten a whiff of something that was not quite right; he felt that my heart was elsewhere. And that perhaps there was a thin crack now forming in his usual self-confidence.

We finished our food in silence, and after we paid and walked out into the wet New York evening, the bright lights all around us suddenly made me feel lonely, almost desperate.

I took Jen's hand and clung to it as if it were the only thing I had left in this world.

FOUR

Gex, 1778

One Friday morning Adele managed to leave the house on her own, which was unusual. When the nanny came to look after Delphine and Yves in the mornings, Adele would take the time to tend to matters of the house—plan meals, make sure the dining rooms were properly cleaned, and check the social schedule for the coming week, so they didn't miss any important engagements. She sometimes went out to the market, always taking someone with her—a maid who could carry the shopping back home. But that morning, she wanted to be alone. She wanted to feel again, even if for a few brief hours, what it was like to be carefree. Neither completely free nor carefree, but she could at least pretend for a short while.

She wore one of her good dresses, a bright mustard-yellow silk fabric with a round décolleté and white lace at the wrists.

"It is the latest fashion in Paris," said the seamstress who made it for her the month before. She had so many dresses to choose from now, alongside a dedicated seamstress who worked with the Bertrand store whenever a customer needed a tailoring job done.

The pretty dresses and the comfortable lifestyle somewhat compensated for what most of the time felt to her like a missed opportunity. A missed opportunity to do something big with her life—travel, read, write. Yes, she was a woman. Yes, she was told again and again that she needed to know her place. But she did not feel comfortable in the role she was pushed into, the role everyone expected her to assume so naturally: that of a wife and a mother.

Had she been a man...had she been a man she would not have married so young. She would have travelled and seen new places. She would have been an adventurer, or a scholar, or both. But as a woman, she did not realize until very recently that the option was even there. Now that she knew that some women indeed became writers, and travelers, and even adventurers— that women *could* indeed do all that, even successfully, she wondered if it was indeed too late. *Or perhaps it wasn't?*

In her own mind she saw herself like Antoinette de Saliès, a writer and philosopher, the founder of a literary society, a woman of influence. But as it was, her life seemed so wasted in this small town, small marriage, unfulfilled dreams of adventure and struggle for the betterment of her country and fellow citizens...

Adele was so caught up in her own thoughts that she nearly walked into someone on the narrow cobbled street. She did not see anyone in front of her when she last looked ahead a few seconds before!

She lost her balance and threw her arms behind her to soften the anticipated fall, but the man she'd nearly crashed into grabbed her shoulders and helped Adele get her balance back. She felt herself blush with embarrassment.

"I am so..." As she started mumbling an apology, she turned her eyes up, and there he was, looking down at her, his hands still holding on to her shoulders.

Jules Badeau. The schoolteacher. The man she has not spoken to in six years, the man who haunted her daydreams as well as the dreams she had at night, whenever she could remember them. He stood before her, his dark eyes serious and sad.

He suddenly let go of her, as if his hands touched fire.

"Are you all right?" he asked. "I did not mean to frighten you."

"I am so sorry..." she said, but he shook his head.

"No, it is me... I shouldn't have."

"Shouldn't have what?" she asked with a small voice, and he hesitated before answering.

"Shouldn't have crossed the street to speak to you, Adele. I know I shouldn't have."

They both stood there, not knowing what to say to each other after all these years. They were well aware of the few people around them, of the inappropriate situation they were putting themselves in. But at that moment, neither of them cared.

"May I walk with you?" asked Jules, and Adele could not find the right words so she just nodded. He walked by her side, a safe distance to her right, in complete silence.

She suddenly became aware of the chirruping of the birds above them; the skies seemed a lighter shade of blue than they were only a few moments before. The commotion of the nearby market seemed to come from far away, and she noticed the smell of fresh bread from the bakery they'd just passed. All her senses were awake; she felt more alive than she had in a long, long time.

"I crossed the street to speak to you," said Jules. "In fact, I've been trying to find you and speak to you for a while now because… I wanted to tell you something. I wanted to tell you that I am leaving Gex."

Adele stopped and turned toward him.

"Where are you going?" she asked softly. *Did she even have the right to ask him such a question,* she wondered.

"Lyon," he said. "For a year, maybe more. I just don't know."

"I heard you're to become a *maître d'armes,*" said Adele before she could stop herself. She was relieved to see a half-smile slowly creep onto Jules' lips.

"You did, did you?"

"Yes, I… I am sorry, it's not that I am following everything you do, but I just…"

"It's all right, Adele," he said in a low voice. "It's all right, it has been a long time, hasn't it?"

She nodded, fighting back tears.

He gently touched her hand, not daring to do more than that to comfort her.

"I was so stupid," she whispered. "I was only eighteen, what did I know?"

He watched her silently for a moment or two. She closed her eyes.

"I am so sorry," she said again.

"I don't want you to be sorry," he said. "I want you to be happy. Are you happy?"

She shook her head but did not answer in words. She could not utter these words, but she knew that he knew.

"You know," he said, "it was my fault too."

She raised her eyes to meet his.

"I now know, I know I should have fought for you. I shouldn't have just let you go and marry someone else without putting up a fight. You were only eighteen, I agree. But I have just one question to ask. May I?"

She nodded, tears overflowing. She took her glove off and wiped them with the back of her hand.

He hesitated. Then took a deep breath, and a step back.

"Would it have made a difference, Adele? Would it have made a difference if I had fought for you?"

Adele looked into his dark eyes, at the face that she once thought was not handsome, but only gentle and kind—and it suddenly seemed to her to be the most beautiful face in the world.

She bit her lip, hesitating over the words that she was going to let out. She knew that once spoken, they could never be taken back. What if this was her only chance? He was leaving for Lyon. Who knew if he'd ever come back? If she didn't speak now, she might never have another chance. A dark cloud moved above them, casting a shadow on them. Was this a sign?

She took a deep breath.

"It would have made a difference, Jules," she finally whispered. "It really would."

He nodded gravely. Then, as if nothing had been said between them, he tipped his hat at her.

"Madame Bertrand," he said in a loud voice, so anyone around who wished to hear their conversation could easily do so. "Have a good day. I shall see you again. *A bientôt.*"

Then, as an afterthought, just before he turned to leave, he said quietly, "I'll be back, Adele. I will be back for you, I promise."

The dark cloud suddenly shifted and the sun shone through again. As she watched him walk away, he stopped for a moment and turned to look at her. She smiled at him and she couldn't be sure, but from a distance she thought that he smiled back.

FIVE

New York, 2018

Jen and I got home around eight. Two empty boxes of pizza and an open, half-drunk bottle of Coke welcomed me in the kitchen. Some of the Coke had spilled onto the counter in a dark, sticky puddle, but no one had bothered to wipe it off.

Jen took one look at my face and went straight to her room, and I walked into the living room to find Don and Tom sitting in front of the TV, watching a basketball match.

I hadn't seen Tom sitting in the living room for months, and on one hand, it was heartwarming to see him next to his father on the sofa. He usually spent most of his time at home locked up in his room, doing homework or chatting to his friends on Snapchat. On the other hand, something about the scene I had walked into simply annoyed me. Why that was, I could not really tell.

"Don't get crumbs all over the sofa," was what I said, and they both looked at me as if I had just come in from outer space.

"Hi, Mom," said Tom.

"Hi Amelia," Don followed.

The truth was that I had become so used to my life without Don, that his mere presence in my space, in what I now considered to be *my* living room, was destabilizing to me. Him sitting there on the sofa, eating his pizza without a plate, kind of got on my nerves.

"Hi," I said to both but to no one in particular, and headed back to the kitchen to clean up the mess they left there.

I then showered and changed into my favorite tights and long-sleeved T-shirt—and sat in front of my computer. It was as if the occurrences of the past few months had released a lot of blockages that I had all my life, and wasn't even aware of. There were so many things bubbling under the surface; so much emotion was bottled up inside of me, and it was not something I could really talk about to anyone I knew. Certainly not Don or Jen or Tom. If the situation were different, perhaps I could have talked about it with Noah, but I could not pick up the phone and call him. What would I say? That I just wanted to talk? Or that I'd made a stupid mistake, which I would now like to try and correct? The fact was that I had made a decision, and now I had to stick with it.

The interesting thing was that I was pretty sure, with some degree of certainty that lay beyond logic and beyond words, it wasn't the first time I'd made this same mistake. But if that was indeed true, I didn't know what to do next and how to get myself out of the repetitive cycle. I felt that only writing could release whatever was eating at me from the inside, even though I had no idea what would be coming up on the screen in front of me if I let my fingers loose.

So I took a small step, and typed: **Premonitions**

SIX

Gex, 1789

It had been over ten years since she last saw him. She had almost given up hope.

Her life, the comfortable life of a wealthy merchant's wife and the mother of his two children, seemed quite hopeless. The hopelessness was not due to something fundamentally wrong with the life she chose, or with her daily existence. It was more that she felt, in a way she could not quite explain to herself or to anyone else, cheated of the real life she hoped she'd have. The feeling of hopelessness was compounded by the fact that her romantic dreams as a young woman—to be helplessly in love with the man she married—were completely shattered.

Neither of the two men in her life—the one she had married and the one she loved, or for that matter, neither her father nor her brother, were expressive men. In nearly twenty years of marriage to Pierre Bertrand, he had never told her that he loved her.

She tried to make their marriage work—she welcomed him into her bed, she had his children. But once the initial excitement of their marriage calmed, there was no effort on his part to make her feel loved or appreciated.

Adele's way of coping with this situation, in which she felt trapped without seeing a way out, was to lock up her heart and throw away the key. And if a feeling of longing, of wanting more than what she had—of wanting to feel love or passion—ever sneaked in, she did her best to ignore it. After all, everyone said she had everything any woman could ever want, didn't they?

The reality was that she and Pierre no longer cared much for each other, and Pierre—that much she knew from the rumors around town—had started caring for another woman. He had a mistress, a young woman of twenty-two, in a neighboring village. Adele never confronted him about it, because her children were young and she had nowhere to go. And even if she did confront him and then leave him—what would she do? And her young children, could they do without their father? Could they do without her?

In a small town like Gex, everyone knew things, almost as soon as they happened. And just as everyone knew about Pierre's mistress, and knew her marriage to Pierre was not a happy one, everyone also knew that a woman alone could not care for two children, and so Adele she took the years as they came, with their ups and downs, comforts and hardships.

Her parents were getting older, and she worried what would happen to them if she left Pierre. Or what would happen to her if anything happened to them. Her parents were considered part of Pierre's family, although throughout the years they continued to be looked down upon, as the poorer relations who had come into the Bertrand family through the back door—through Adele's marriage to Pierre.

As it was, Pierre made sure that Adele's parents were comfortable in their old age, for he could not let his parents-in-law seem uncared for. For that, she could not fault him, and was grateful for the relative comfort they all lived in.

But Adele also heard other rumors, rumors about Jules Badeau. The rumors were rare and unreliable, but they indicated that he became a successful man in Lyon. She heard Monsieur Voltaire appreciated and trusted him, and often sent for him when he wanted to consult him. She heard Jules had never married. But rumors were rumors. What the reality of his life in Lyon was, she did not truly know.

Then, nearly a decade after Jules left, Adele received a note.

It was delivered with great secrecy in the late hours of the morning when Pierre was at the store. A messenger, a teenage boy she'd never seen before, knocked on the door and asked to see Madame Bertrand. When she came to the door, he put the note in her hand, bowed to her and immediately ran without waiting for her to read the note, or reply to it.

"Meet me tomorrow at noon, where we first met," was all it said. Nothing more. It was not signed, but she recognized the handwriting. She knew immediately —he'd come back, just like he had promised he would.

The next morning, as soon as Pierre left for the store, Adele picked up a basket.

"I am going to the market, and shall be lunching in town," she said to Julie, the new day-maid.

"I will come along and carry the shopping, *madame*," Julie was quick to offer.

"Thank you, it won't be necessary today," Adele said, and felt her cheeks flushing. She hurried out the door and disappeared, clutching her basket, leaving behind a baffled young maid.

Adele had been back to that very place many times over the past ten years. In her fancy, she'd walk there and see Jules waiting for her, as if some kind of bond tied them in long-distance, invisible knots, and he could sense her desperation with the life she had created for herself.

Every time she'd get there, she would stop, take in the fresh air and the familiar sight of the town of Gex beneath her, sit on the rock not far from when she'd lost her way nearly twenty years before, and cry.

She did not dare cry at home, for there was always someone around—the children, the maids, Pierre. And it was not as if she had had any valid reason to cry—at least not in the eyes of others.

"You should be grateful for the good life you have," her

mother said to her at every opportunity. And she was right. She should be grateful. But she wasn't.

As she approached the very spot where she had sat many times over the past ten years, she stopped, stood still and closed her eyes. She feared that she would, once again, be disappointed, be disillusioned, when she saw the empty rock.

But then, then, she opened her eyes and walked a few more steps. And there he was, sitting on her rock, just like in her many daydreams over the past decade. There he was, not very different from how she remembered him. A little older, his hair grayer, thinner, his clothes considerably more fashionable than the way he was dressed when they first met. But there was no mistaking, it was him. Jules Badeau was waiting for her, the real Jules Badeau, not the Jules of her dreams, and that was quite a different story altogether.

Adele had to summon all her willpower to stop herself from throwing her arms around him. She knew that if she did, if she found that place within herself deep enough and dark enough to throw everything else to the wind and fly into Jules arms, she would never be able to turn back.

Instead, she quietly sat on the rock, by his side, careful not to touch him.

SEVEN

West Africa, 1577

He was numb with fear. As the witchdoctor's apprentice, he did not have many opportunities to engage in acts of bravery. The other village boys would always compete with each other, constantly trying to prove they were courageous and tough young men. From early childhood—he wasn't quite sure how young—the apprentice knew. He knew that his fate was tied to that of his teacher, his master, his mentor, the childless witchdoctor, in ways he would never be able to explain. The old man saved his life when he was just an infant, and he was indebted to him in many ways—ways he would not be able to understand until, until...until perhaps it was too late.

And now, was it too late?

He heard the explosions. He could still feel the smoke stinging his eyes, infiltrating his lungs, filling his mouth with the bitter taste of ash. He could hear his own heartbeat—that was what scared him most, as he was certain *they* could hear it too.

Soon after the old man left the hut, the apprentice sneaked back in. The old man sent him into the forest to look after his mother and the other women and children who hid there. There was no point in sending him to join the other village men, the warriors. He was never a warrior, he was an apprentice medicine man, *and as such,* said the old man, *his services were just as important as those of the young warriors, and would be needed afterward.*

Afterward? After what? He wanted to ask, but he didn't. And now he could guess. No, now he actually understood.

The bloodcurdling screams and smoke that entered the hut like an uninvited phantom—a mix of burning wood and roasting flesh—came from the direction of the village. They did not leave much room for doubt. Those horrible men, those white-faced devils with their machines that could kill from afar, and their sharp blades that could kill from a short distance too, overcame the brave village warriors, armed only with courage, spears, bows and arrows. Part of him wanted to sneak out of the hut, to go and see what was happening in the village. But another part of him would not allow his legs to move.

This was the first time he had disobeyed his mentor. He did not go into the forest, he did not look after the women and children as instructed. Instead, he lingered nearby; he stayed where he could observe the hut, until he saw the old man come out, dressed in his ceremonial garments. He wore a ridiculously large headdress—the one passed on to him by his forefathers—made of rich cloth and colored feathers in faded hues of red and yellow, which looked as if they'd served in many ceremonies before. He shuffled his feet toward the village as if this was his last journey on this earth. As if he knew it beyond doubt.

That was when the apprentice tiptoed back into the hut, and curled into a ball in one corner. He did not want to leave the old man alone to face the evil ones. But, he also did not want to die today. He was not ready. He still had more work to do—even the shaman acknowledged it—and the old man knew about these things, he knew what was best.

The young man took a deep breath and peeked out of the hut. He could see nothing, hear nothing. Even the birds were silent now.

After a while that seemed like a lifetime—bent down low—he left the hut. Slowly walking along the tree line, he was careful not to make any noise or raise any dust, for who knew what those evil men might be up to now.

As he approached the village huts, the sun disappeared and a massive cloud drifted in from the west. It was as if it sought to cover the sun completely, to save the eyes of the young man from the horrors he was about to witness.

The wind had picked up and the foliage around him rustled. That was when the birds and animals could be heard again, or perhaps it was he who did not pay attention before? No, he was certain, it was *his* doing, his master calling the elements to his aid. The terrifying dark magic he had been referring to not that long ago—the dark side of his craft for which he'd had to cross the invisible line. But where was *he* now?

EIGHT

Foothills of the Jura, near Gex, 1789

Adele knew she had to avoid the question she really wanted to ask. She didn't think she had the right to ask it—to ask Jules what took him so long to come back.

"I heard you were close to the late Monsieur Voltaire," she said quietly instead. They were walking in the mountains, the foothills of the Jura—not far from the place where some twenty years before Jules had found her wandering on her own, nearly frozen to death; where, two decades earlier, his dog—whose name she could not recall now—licked her hands and her face and brought her back from the clutches of desperation to the warm eyes and arms of the man who was now walking by her side. Then, he was a simple schoolteacher—dressed like a peasant—in rough fabric and a sensible but old winter coat. Now he looked like a city person, his earth-colored *justaucorps* sitting nicely over his light waistcoat and breeches. She could not help but admire his perfectly knotted cravat.

He looked at her, his face serious. He looked older than she remembered him—but she found his face even more handsome as he aged. *What did he think of her,* she wondered. *Had she changed much in the years he was gone?*

"I owe Monsieur Voltaire a great debt of gratitude, which I will never be able to repay," he said. "I tried to do so in his last years, when he took me in as one of his secretaries in Ferney. He always referred to it as Fernex, the old way it was pronounced, of course. I was fortunate enough to listen and take down some of his dictations, as he was particularly appreciative of my handwriting. But I have not yet succeeded in repaying even a fraction of my debt to him, nor in keeping my promise to him to work for his cause. My moral debt to him is indeed eternal, but I shall soon endeavor to repay at least some of it."

She waited for more, but he didn't seem to want to offer it willingly.

"Why is your debt to him so great?" she finally asked.

He sighed.

"He helped me find a purpose in life when I could find none. He took me in and gave me not only work but also a reason to live, when my heart was broken and everything else seemed meaningless," he said briefly, his voice low, as if he were already saying too much.

She didn't dare ask why—why was his heart broken.

Was it because of her choice to marry Pierre? However, thanks to her choice to marry Pierre, because of that choice he had the good fortune to spend time with Monsieur Voltaire. She could still not believe that he had attained such a high position, had so much luck, and taken part in such glamorous work.

Would it have made a difference? she wondered. Would it have made a difference to her family had Jules been in the service of Monsieur Voltaire back then? Would they have then not pushed her to marry Pierre, who was a good man and a good provider— her mother was right about that part. But Pierre had never encouraged her to go beyond her role as a wife and mother, a role that somehow did not at all make her happy. And when she did try to live a little beyond what he thought to be her duty to him and the children, he always objected. And she…she felt as if her life so far had been wasted.

But now, now that Jules is back…

Jules looked up at a bird, a black redstart, flying over their heads. They both stood still, admiring the small creature.

Jules then looked straight at her, searching for her eyes, for the first time in many years.

"Adele," he said.

"Yes?"

"There is a reason I asked you to take this walk with me today. There is a reason I came back from Lyon after such a long absence. And perhaps I shouldn't have asked you to walk with me, but I had to speak to you in private. I did not want to follow you on the street again, and make you uncomfortable. It is just not done."

"You said you'd come back," she said. "And now you're back."

"There's more to it," he said. "I am back, but..."

She waited for him to continue.

They walked for a few more moments in silence, before he was ready to speak again.

"I am leaving for Paris soon, Adele. In a few days; a week at most. I now need to keep a promise I made to Monsieur Voltaire before he died. Now is the right time to try and...and work for his cause. I wanted to tell you this personally, for I do not know if I will return here again after concluding the affairs in Paris, they are not simple ones. But I wanted to keep my promise to you, too—and I promised I would be back."

She felt her throat closing; tears welled up in her eyes.

He touched her hand.

"What's the matter?" he asked, his voice hardly more than a whisper.

"I wish you didn't have to go away again," she said. "Although what right do I have to ask this of you?"

He sighed.

"There were moments over the past fifteen years when I would have done anything to hear those words from you, Adele. But now...now, there is not much that can be done. You have your life, and I guess that finally, I will now get mine, even if I have to sacrifice it for...for a greater cause."

She looked at him, not sure what to make of his words.

"What do you mean?" she asked. "What kind of sacrifice?"

He hesitated.

"These are important times, Adele. Times of change, just like Monsieur Voltaire hoped. He always spoke of that Englishman, the English *philosophe*, Francis Bacon. He spoke of science and knowledge, of utility and of progress. Monsieur Voltaire would read his texts out loud, and envisioned a change in our *Patrie*, in our land. And so, although he was old and frail by then, he had us, his humble friends and assistants, promise we would work tirelessly to achieve progress for our glorious France, Adele. This is why I must go to Paris now."

She covered her face with her hands.

What right do I have to say anything? She thought. *What right do I have to demand anything from this man, this man who could have been my husband, this man I sent away like an unwanted suitor. This kind, magnificent man whom I loved so much, whom I still love so much. This man who looks to achieve things for the greater good, not for himself.*

"I am sorry," she said. "I have no right."

"You always wanted to go to Paris," he said. "Have you ever been to Paris?"

She shook her head, fighting back the tears.

"Would you come with me, then?" he asked quietly.

Time slowed down. She heard that bird. Was it the same redstart—or maybe it was a chaffinch. She couldn't really tell, but it was chirruping as if its life depended on it, as if it was trying to deliver her an important message.

The trees—how come there were so many leaves on them already? It was almost spring but she hadn't noticed all these fresh leaves until now. The long grass, it was caressed by the wind with such grace...

What did he say? Did he really ask her to go with him? To Paris?

"I know you can't come," he then said quietly. "Of course. you can't. But just once, I needed to ask."

NINE

New York, 2018

"Why do I always choose the wrong partners?" sighed Lauren, my editorial assistant.

Her eyes were red from another sleepless night, or maybe from crying in the bathroom. Yet another breakup from another boyfriend—I've counted five such devastating breakups since she's been working for me in the past three years. And there were a few less devastating ones in between, just guys who "were not right" for her or "didn't get what she was all about."

"It's not only you," I said. "It's most of us."

Lauren was in her late twenties, dark hair, green eyes, a bit chubby. She had great enthusiasm for dating, for yoga, and for various strange spiritual rituals—she would tell me in detail (if I had the time and will to listen) about how she cleared the energies in her apartment after ending this or that relationship, with fresh water and precisely nine slices of orange, while chanting some mantra. She had me repeat "On Mani Padme Hum" several times, claiming it would allow us both to get rid of negative energies that drew us to the wrong people.

I had other ideas about why we were attracted to the wrong people.

"It's because we are fucked up, and they are fucked up, but the things we are fucked up about are not complementary," I said. "If we found the person that complements our imperfections, we'd be much better off. No amount of water or orange juice sprinkled around the room can change that."

Lauren gave this some consideration.

"You've been in one relationship for the last twenty years," she said. "Maybe they're not all the same. Not everyone is fucked up, are they? Maybe it's just that we are all on different journeys, here to learn different things. To settle some of our different karmic debts."

A year ago, I would have laughed at this analysis, but my recent experiences with hypnotherapy, where I'd seen the life of Adele, a young woman in eighteenth-century France, and that of a shaman protecting his village in the early days of the slave-trade in Africa, kind of blew my mind. I hadn't shared this shift in perspective with anyone, because I didn't know anyone who'd actually get it without thinking I'd lost it following the breakup of my marriage to Don. I couldn't really share this with Lauren, either. She was my assistant and eighteen years my junior. But I suddenly found myself listening more attentively to what before I had thought was a heap of mumbo-jumbo. I found my mind slowly opening to the slight possibility that some of the things she talked about might have some inexplicable truth in them, especially after my recent trip to Southeast France, when I discovered that some of the places I saw during my hypnosis sessions and in my dreams actually existed and were not a complete figment of my sleep-deprived imagination.

"Maybe," was all I could muster.

Lauren eyed me suspiciously.

"Oh," she said. "You're not looking at me as if I am slightly mad, talking about spiritual journeys and karmic debts. What happened?"

"Nothing," I said, but my voice must have been somewhat defensive because she suddenly had a wide smile on her face, her red-rimmed eyes now sparkling.

"Amelia, are you in love?"

"What a ridiculous idea," I said.

"I noticed a big change in you in the last month," she said. "After you and Don broke up, I was so worried about you, you were depressed for an entire year. Have you met someone new?

43

Or are you back with Don?"

I sighed. There was no point in pretending—Lauren was eighteen years younger, and my assistant, but she might very well be the only person vaguely able to understand what I was currently going through.

"Both," I said.

TEN

Gex, 1789

"How can I come with you to Paris, Jules?" Adele finally said. "I would like to, more than anything, but how can I? There's Pierre, and the children, Yves and Delphine..."

"The children are grown up now," he said. "They are fourteen, fifteen?"

She nodded. He was right. They were not children anymore; they were young adults. Pierre and his family could care for them. She would not disappear completely from their lives, although of course they might never want to see her again if she embarrassed the family in such a way. But for once, just for once in her life, she felt that she needed to follow her heart, no matter what others might think, say or do.

"I waited, you know," he said. "I waited many, many years to ask you this question. It is not in my character to suggest something so...so daring for you. It is the main reason I did not come back sooner. I had to find that place within myself that was willing to throw everything to the wind and ask this question, regardless of what the answer would be. I also knew that your children needed you. But tell me about Pierre. How do you feel about Pierre?"

Adele felt the words clamoring for space; she did not want to let them out. How could she tell Jules, how could she tell him about Pierre without sounding ungrateful, treacherous, childish? How could she even begin describing the long days, and the silent nights, and the heartache that came with this marriage? How could she speak of the regrets, too numerous to even begin counting? The pointlessness of it all, the feeling that time slipped through her fingers like sand in an hourglass, that even the regrets only grew as time passed.

Yes, Pierre turned out to be a good provider, but she did not love him. She didn't really love him when she married him. And love did not grow in their relationship, like many had suggested all those years ago, before she had married him. She didn't think he really loved her either. He gave her the feeling that this marriage was somewhat beneath him; that marrying her was a foolish impulse that he was willing to see through. Indeed, she fell in love with a promise of a glamorous life, a promise that he never kept. She fell in love with the idea of sharing her life with a man who would want to go places—and take her with him. Pierre did not even let her go to work in the family store; he truly believed that all she was good for was caring for the children and the house—and even then, she failed him by not doing a very good job of it.

Adele knew about Pierre's affairs. He kept one, if not two, mistresses. Everyone knew about them, yet Adele never confronted him, for what would she say to him?

She could not give him the love he wanted, neither the emotional love nor the physical love that he surely deserved from a wife. And the truth was, she didn't really care. She was ridden with guilt, with remorse, with self-doubt. But she could not tell Jules all that. Besides, he probably already knew on one level or another. Somehow, she was convinced that he knew. Otherwise, he wouldn't have asked.

They stood in silence. The silence was so complete, even the birds stopped their chatter, as if they knew a heavy matter was being weighed just beneath them.

The journey to Paris was to take eight days. Jules said he would be back for her in the third week of May. If Adele was indeed coming with him, he said, he would delay his trip. He wanted to make sure all his business is settled in the region, for he did not know when he would be back next.

"Perhaps I will never be welcome back in Gex," he said. "But I can live with that. I shall make peace with it. Besides, you will love Paris in the early summer, Adele."

Adele visited her elderly parents a few days before the secret departure. She couldn't leave without saying her goodbyes, even if they were not official goodbyes.

"Papa, I love you," she said as she served him his tea and was surprised when he smiled at her wearily and refused the tea.

"It is too hot to drink tea, *ma fille*", he said, exhausted. The temperatures that late spring were unusually high and caused her father ill health. He still went out to the fields in the mornings, but by noon he'd be back home, ready for lunch and a rest that lasted until the late hours of the afternoon. He would then not leave home again until early the next morning, when it was cool again for a few hours.

That spring there was a severe drought all over France, and she knew that her father was worried about his crops, although—growing their own produce—her parents would at least have enough food to eat, if not to sell to others.

"I am glad we don't have to worry about you and your children," said her mother that day. "We will be fine. Your father merely needs more rest in this unbearably hot weather."

Adele wanted to say something meaningful to her mother but could not find the words. She knew that her mother loved her very much, and she undoubtedly loved her mother—but she could not find it in her heart to completely forgive Anne Durand for what she felt was an ill-advised and unhappy marriage, although she now realized that some of that was her own doing. Her heart was never really free to love Pierre Bertrand and she, Adele, never tried to change that. *If I tell her now,* thought Adele, *if I tell her of my intentions, she will try to stop me.*

Anne Durand looked at her daughter as if she knew.

"Is all in order, Adele?" she asked, her eyes two narrow slits.

Adele slowed down and sighed. She knew there was an unusual bounce in her step and she had tried hard to stop smiling to herself over the past few days, fearing people would notice. In her mid-thirties, she now felt eighteen again, and worried it was showing.

"*Oui, maman,*" she said. "Everything is fine."

She guessed her mother had heard that the schoolteacher, now a fully qualified *maître-d'armes*, had returned to Gex from Lyon a couple of weeks back. She worried that Anne Durand would make the connection between this fact and the newly found color in her daughter's cheeks. *But does it really matter? I'll be gone tomorrow anyway and the whole town will be talking about me for weeks,* she thought.

Having an affair outside her marriage—although she could hardly call it that at this early stage, as the only part of Jules she had ever touched were his hands—suddenly felt exciting. It was an *affaire de coeur,* an affair of the heart—for her heart completely belonged to Jules Badeau. Now, looking back, she realized it probably always had belonged to him, since the day he found her on the mountain. That was the reason there was not much room in her heart for Pierre, and to a lesser extent, not as much room for her children, as she would have liked.

As long as they depended on her—Pierre, and their two children—she was there for them. But now, now things were different. They no longer needed her, and she needed...she needed to live the life she always wanted to live, or at least to try.

The kind of excitement she was feeling was the excitement she had longed for all of her life, a life so far spent first as an obedient daughter who married the man her family wanted her to marry, and then as a mother and a wife. That was about to end. She was going to escape to Paris, where kings and courtesans had affairs, where couples could live in sin without risking contempt from those around them.

"The winds of revolution are blowing in Paris," whispered

Jules before they parted a few days before, agreeing to meet on Friday morning, to start the journey to Paris together, toward a new life. "This undeserving buffoon who calls himself Louis XVI, is the final descendent in a family that has brought our glorious country to its knees. And I made a promise to monsieur Voltaire before his death, a promise I must keep."

He would not say more, but that was enough to fill Adele's imagination with heroic acts that Jules, with her by his side, would commit in Paris.

She still remembered the dinner at her parents' house, this very same place where she was now trying to find a way to say goodbye—as she didn't know if she would ever be allowed back after the embarrassment she would cause her family, her parents, her children. It was nearly two decades ago that Jules had sat at the very table she was now caressing with her fingertips. He sat right there, between her father and her mother, and across from her, Adele.

She recalled the conversation as if it happened yesterday: her father complained about King Louis XV, who according to him was not only fat and ten times worse than a lowly thief but also a selfish coward. Jules Badeau just smiled, and did not let himself be dragged into slandering their monarch, but quietly mentioned that it was strange, in his opinion, that Monsieur Durand chose to name his only son after a king he disliked so much. The memory of this witty observation made Adele smile even now, nearly twenty years later, but she quickly covered her mouth when she saw her mother staring at her.

"Something is going on, Adele," said Anne Durand. "I have not seen you in such a pleasant mood for years."

Adele lowered her eyes and clenched her fists, determined not to give anything away.

She still had to pack—although she intended to take as little as possible so as to leave unnoticed. She would need a few dresses, one or two *chemises* to wear as undergarments, a couple of hats, and two or three pairs of shoes, no more. And of course, one thing she would not leave behind would be the blue-gray dress, the same one her mother spent many hours making out of the wonderful fabric Jules gifted her for her eighteenth birthday. In a way, it was because of this fabric that she had let her mother convince her into marrying Pierre Bertrand. It was at his shop that she first touched the magnificent material, on a sunny morning in June when she went with her mother to look for fabric to make a dress for her eighteenth birthday party.

Her mother insisted on buying a dull yellow chiffon, which she said was more "practical," but Adele had really wanted the blue-gray silk, which she knew was the latest fashion in Paris all those years ago. Her mother won the argument of course, as she held the authority and also the purse. They walked out with the ugly yellow fabric, which then turned in her mother's expert hands into a beautiful dress for Adele's eighteenth birthday party, celebrated at Madame Montagne's barn.

"A husband who can take my daughter to Paris would surely be able to buy her fabric for a new dress," said her mother back then, and Adele still remembered the embarrassment she felt when Pierre, then the young and stylish town merchant's son, said he'd be honored to take Adele to Paris one day.

"Don't be silly, your family would never agree," said Anne Durand to Pierre Bertrand, the wealthy merchant's son, but when the glorious blue-gray silk appeared on Adele's doorstep a week later, they thought that maybe they would.

Maybe Pierre Bertrand's well-off family would not mind if he married a farmer's daughter after all, they thought, and everyone around her was excited about Adele's prospects—so excited that even she, Adele, got carried away in the general enthusiasm and agreed to marry him. Now, eighteen years later, she was about to leave him for the man she could have married. The man she *should* have married. Jules Badeau, the schoolteacher.

ELEVEN

New York, 2018

I went to pick Jen up from the Manhattan Fencing Center after work, and saw Noah there. He was giving an individual lesson to one of the younger kids, a boy who was half his size, but very quick on his feet.

"Do you mind waiting a few minutes?" I asked Jen, and she smiled a conspiratorial smile at me.

"Can I have money for a hot chocolate? I'll wait at the café on Thirty-eighth," she offered.

I fumbled in my purse and handed her a ten-dollar bill, then sat on the bench and watched Noah coach the boy—I could see him over the counter that separated the *salle* from the waiting area.

Noah finished the lesson and then tried to walk past me as if he hadn't seen me—but he stood no chance.

"Hi," I said. "How are you?"

What I really wanted to say was—*please help me save myself from the mistake I am currently making.* But I figured I had to start somewhere more sensible.

"Fine," he said. "And you?"

Damn you, I wanted to say. *Damn you for being so accepting, so distant, so indifferent. Damn you for coming into my life and turning everything upside down, and letting me walk away as if none of it mattered.*

"I'm okay," I said. "Sort of. I wanted to talk to you."

"You are talking to me," he said.

"I meant, not here. Can we talk somewhere else, not here? Another time? Soon?"

He looked me in the eye for the first time since we'd spoken on the phone a few weeks before, since I told him I was going back to Don.

"Okay," he said.

"How about tomorrow morning?" I suggested. "Before work. Coffee."

"Okay," he said again. "Tell me where and I'll be there."

The next morning we met at a new place, not far from my office. Noah shifted in his chair because he didn't like new places, especially if they were crowded. They made him feel uncomfortable. I shifted in my chair because I didn't like the position I'd put myself into—sitting across from him without knowing how to say what I really wanted to say.

"You wanted to talk," he said.

"Yes," I said. "I am just not sure how to say it, because it sounds a bit crazy."

He looked at me, and I noticed he hadn't shaved that day— his face had dark stubble that made him look distant and secretive—as if he had something to hide.

"Do you believe in past lives?" I asked.

He looked at me without saying anything.

"Well, do you?"

"No." he finally said. "I believe that life is a series of man-made or evolutionary experiences and then we die, usually regretfully. But how does this have anything to do with what you want to say to me?"

"It's complicated," I started. "But I feel that we have some kind of karmic connection that is beyond just a relationship that happened, or will happen, or won't."

He continued staring at me. I suspected he enjoyed making me feel uncomfortable.

"I know I sound weird saying that," I said. "I even sound weird to myself. But you know, when I was in France something really strange happened. And it had to do with you, I think."

He still didn't say anything.

"So here's the really bizarre thing I wanted to ask you," I said, gathering all my courage. "Will you come with me to France, and help me figure it out?"

A muscle twitched in his jaw, but other than that his face remained expressionless.

"With or without your ex-husband?" he then asked, looking the other way.

I smiled at him. I just couldn't help myself—it was something about his matter-of-fact tone of voice that completely won me over.

"Please, Noah. This is something I really need to figure out, otherwise my life will never go back to normal."

"Are you serious?" he asked.

I nodded.

"I can't really explain this in a way that will make sense to you, or to me, here in this café. Or even here in New York. But if you come with me to Gex, if you come with me…maybe you'll understand. Maybe we can figure this out together."

He took a sip of the coffee in front of him.

"When?"

"As soon as we can both take a week off work, I suppose," I said.

He looked at me as if I just materialized in front of his eyes from thin air.

"Amelia, does this sound normal to you?" he said. "First, you're telling me that you are leaving me to go back to your husband, and then you're asking me to take a week off work and come with you to France? And I am the one supposedly lacking in social skills. Don't you think this is just a little confusing?"

"Noah, please trust me, just this once. I know it doesn't make much sense to you. It doesn't make sense to me either, but if you can trust me and come along, we both might understand it better. I am not suggesting that we go as a couple. We'll get separate rooms. We can even get separate flights if you prefer. But I owe it to myself, and to you, to have this figured out. Okay?"

He stared at me, speechless.

"Okay," he finally said.

TWELVE

Gex, 1789

Adele slipped out of the house unnoticed, after Pierre had left for the store the next morning. Yves went with his father as Pierre expected a particularly busy day, with new merchandise arriving from Paris.

"Would you like to come in and help me, Adele?" he asked the previous evening, and Adele thought she would faint. In eighteen years of marriage, she'd asked him again and again to allow her to help him at the store. She had told him that it would give her a break from the tedious chores and mundane existence that involved caring for the house and for the children. But Pierre had never agreed.

"Someone has to look after the house and the children, I can look after the store," he had said again and again, and so Adele stopped asking.

But now, he was actually asking for her help in receiving the merchandise from Paris.

"I am sorry, Pierre, I've planned to meet with Eugenie," said Adele faintly. The truth was she had not seen her friend Eugenie for many weeks, and a meeting between them was long overdue.

"Oh," said Pierre. "I thought you'd be happy to come and help. You always say how much you'd like to work at the store."

"Yes," whispered Adele, fighting back the lump in her throat. "Maybe another time."

"Very well," said Pierre, matter-of-factly. "Yves, you will come with me then. You need to get into the store business anyway. After all, it will be yours one day."

Adele sighed in relief.

And as soon as Pierre and Yves left the house in the morning, she sent Delphine to her mother-in-law's house.

"Delphine, *grande-maman* is not well. She needs your help this morning," she said to her daughter. Her heart ached, yet she knew that the two women—her daughter and her mother-in-law, got along very well. The elderly Madame Bertrand would be more than happy to care for Mademoiselle Bertrand, her teenage granddaughter. She would be even more glad to be proven right, after all these years, about the unreliable and treacherous character of her daughter-in-law, Adele.

"Delphine is from our side of the family," Pierre's mother always said. "Look, she has my eyes and sharp brains."

Delphine not only had her grandmother's eyes and sharp brains, but also her inflexible personality, thought Adele. She probably even said it once or twice to Delphine herself. Her daughter would just look at her with disapproving eyes, as if she already knew—even as a young child—that in the future, her mother would leave her husband and her teenage children to run away to Paris with another man.

And so, when her husband and son left the house to go to the store, and her daughter left to assist her grandmother, Adele took out a small suitcase—the same one she brought with her when she had moved into this very house some eighteen years back—and started folding clothes into it. She hesitated between her many dresses, and ended up choosing three, which she thought would serve her best in Paris. The first to go in the case was the blue-gray one her mother had made for her from Jules Badeau's fabric. She added a couple of other dresses, a pair of shoes, and just a little jewelry—her daughter could have the rest. She then closed the case, prepared her travel cloak which she had especially made some fifteen years ago, but had never used until now, and sat down to do the hardest thing of all: to write the letter saying goodbye to her old life.

When the carriage stopped in front of the house an hour later, she was waiting by the front door. She had sent the two maids into town, giving them a long shopping list that would take at least two hours to complete.

The street was deserted, as if some kind of divine intervention had stepped in to make sure that Adele would be able to leave unnoticed, at least for a few more hours.

When Jules Badeau stepped down and helped her into the carriage, and the coachman tied her case on top, she felt as if she was following an old script—irrational, irresponsible, irreversible—but nonetheless written somewhere in her life plan.

THIRTEEN

New York, 2018

The flight from JFK to Geneva was planned to take just under eight hours, but those eight hours made me understand the concept of the elasticity of time.

I took a taxi to the airport after a strained farewell from Don, who knew something was not quite right.

"When will you be back?" he asked, and I rolled my eyes.

"A week, just like I told you. You can manage looking after the kids for a week, can't you? They can pretty much look after themselves these days."

"Sure, I can," he said. "It's you I am worried about. You don't seem right."

"I am actually fine," I said. "I am working on my second novel and I need to find some things out. And frankly, I need some time away."

He didn't say anything—things had been pretty strained between us over the past couple of weeks. He broke up with Claudette, but I knew she was still calling him. I actually felt bad for her, although I could not deny that it also felt good on a certain level—that even though I was not really convinced I actually wanted Don back, at least she got her just desserts for taking him from his family.

I didn't speak to Noah in the weeks before our trip, but I knew he was far from happy with the way I handled things. He would have liked me to tell Don that I was going with him, but I was reluctant to tell Don that Noah was coming along on my research trip—I knew it would add a lot of stress to the planning of the trip, maybe even prevent it altogether. But I also knew that I was finally free from my chains as a wife, a mother, a woman. I was an individual looking to find their path in life, even if from the outside this trip could look as if I was taking a week away with a former lover.

Noah was neither a former lover, nor a future lover. He was a man holding the key to my understanding of life, of myself and yes, he was also holding the key to the novel I was currently working on, and that—even if it didn't matter to Don—mattered immensely to me.

I met Noah at the boarding gate after not having seen him for about a month—and I almost didn't recognize him. He'd lost weight and had dark circles around his eyes. I could feel my own heart thumping as I approached him.

"Hi," I said.

"So you haven't changed your mind," he said.

"No," I said. "Why would I? Did you?"

"I'm here, ain't I?" he said.

It took nearly four weeks for me to clear the trip with work, and with Don. Noah also needed that time to organize taking a week off work, to get other coaches to take over his lessons and his competition travel. During that period, we communicated briefly by abrupt text messages, as if every letter we typed cost us a day out of our lives.

And then we sat next to each other on the plane, but did not exchange any words.

Something ancient stood between us—I could only define it as apprehension, hesitation, even fear.

Noah was guarded, silent, brooding. And I did not know how to breach the very tangible bubble of protection he'd put around himself. We were like two strangers who used to be lovers, or lovers about to become strangers. One way or another, over three hours passed before Noah spoke.

"So when are you going to tell me why you've asked me to

come with you to France?" he asked.

I didn't answer at first, but then I felt I had to.

"Now, if you'd like. I just worry that you won't believe me."

"Did Don believe you when you said you were going on another work trip?" he asked.

I shrugged.

"I think it's pretty obvious to Don that he can't tell me what to do or not to do these days," I said. "It's not about him for a change, you know. This time it's all about me."

He didn't say anything.

"Why are you so angry with me?" I asked. "You knew I was still married, at least officially, didn't you? I told you that Don and I were separated, that he lived with another woman. I couldn't predict that things would turn out this way. Don and I hadn't been living together for almost a year when you and I met—and we hadn't been occupying the same planet for about a decade."

Noah glanced at me sideways.

"Tell me then," he said.

"Okay," I said and took a deep breath.

"Remember when you nearly ran me over, when we met all those months ago? When we met again after high school twenty years earlier, I mean. Well, that was a life-changing day for me. Not only did our paths cross after more than two decades, but something else happened to me... Something spiritual, for lack of a better word. I was on my way out from a hypnotherapy session when you nearly flattened me. I was so focused on my own thoughts I wasn't really paying attention. But I now believe that the timing was far from coincidental. To understand it better, to even be able to explain it better, I have to go back to France."

I took his hand and he didn't pull away. We just sat there, holding hands for a while.

Then he pulled his hand away and stared out the window for the rest of the flight. And I fell asleep, but didn't dare put my head on his shoulder, even though it was barely ten inches away.

FOURTEEN

West Africa, 1577

The young man realized immediately that some of the huts were on fire, the burning wood and straw crackling, consumed by the orange flames. Fire! He needed to put it out somehow. But how, on his own? Him, a cowardly boy, an apprentice medicine man, how could he succeed if all the brave warriors had failed?

He needed help; he needed help more than ever before in his entire life. He felt useless; as if he was a lowly despicable person for hiding in the hut, disobeying his teacher's instructions and too afraid to go and help him in his struggle against the white-faced ghost-men.

Now finally he found the courage to try to do something to help—but as the young man approached the baobab stump in the center of the village, he noticed a human body. At once, he recognized the feathered headdress that lay on the corpse of the shaman, like a bird with a life of its own. A living bird-head on a dead human body. Something about that headdress made his blood run cold.

Then he heard what sounded like a low moan coming from one of the huts. He tried to identify which hut the sound came from. It was half human, half animal, and, like the headdress, not dead—but not completely alive either.

He nearly stepped on a mangled body as he made his way to the hut from which he thought the sound had originated—and as if in passing, he noticed it was Mululu, a boy his age he'd known all his life. Except, it did not look like Mululu; it looked like an empty shell in the form of Mululu, skin charred and blood spilling out of his mouth, painting the earth black.

The wind stopped and fat drops of rain started falling from the darkening skies—rain, now? It never rained in the afternoon. Never, except…was this the help he was hoping for?

The heavy drops of rain turned into a downpour, a ferocious and sudden downpour that put out the fire as it descended on the burning huts in streams as large as waterfalls. He took shelter in one of the huts and strained to try and make out any sounds, but none could be heard above the noise of the downpour.

And the rainstorm, this unexpected and unusual rainstorm, stopped as suddenly as it had started, moments after the fire had been put out, leaving behind drenched huts, a sizzle of smoke and dark, wet soil.

He left the hut again, a little more confident now, as it seemed that the evil white ghost-men had left. But what they left in their wake was incomprehensible.

Dozens of bodies, young men, lay on the ground, mangled, wet, dead. He could not see any women or children.

They must had all hid in the forest, he thought. But by the baobab stump he saw his mentor, his beloved teacher, the body of an old man, lifeless. Even the headdress was now all drenched. It did not look alive anymore, as if the sudden storm had sucked the life force from it. He gently removed it from the shaman's head and tried to rearrange the ruffled feathers.

And then, his face wet with rain and tears, he headed into the forest, to try and find the rest of his people. To find someone who could help him bury the dead.

FIFTEEN

Geneva, 1789

The small private coach Jules had arranged for, took them from Gex to Sécheron, near Geneva—a pleasant ride that took just over an hour. They were to mount the weekly *grande diligence* coach, headed for Paris, at one o'clock that afternoon.

"We'll have time for a light meal," said Jules and guided her into the small inn. The large *diligence* carriage was already out front, a young man brushing the horses and another polishing the carriage until he could see his face reflecting in it.

They took lunch together, a bowl of soup and freshly baked bread.

"Not hungry?" asked Jules, smiling his reserved smile, and Adele noticed that she was indeed playing with her spoon instead of eating her soup.

"I am sorry, I am too nervous to eat," she admitted. "I feel like I am eighteen again and you're invited to lunch with us."

Jules laughed.

"So much has happened since then, Adele," he said. "That feels as if it happened in a different lifetime."

For a moment she thought he was going to move his hand and touch hers, but then he changed his mind. The first step was the hardest.

Jules looked at her silently, his eyes saying everything he didn't say in words.

"Try to eat, we have a long journey until we stop to sup," he finally said.

She did.

Twenty minutes later they boarded the large shiny carriage,

the horses pawing at the ground restlessly, eager to get going.

There were four other passengers on board, all well-dressed men, their wigs well fitted and their bright-colored coats made of expensive velvet. They all appeared to be travelling to Paris on business, and Adele sat very close to Jules, by the window, and kept her eyes down. She feared they'd notice her sweaty palms and hear her wildly fluttering heart. She feared they'd wonder about her, wonder who she was and why was she, a simple woman, going to Paris. Could they see how excited she was about this trip, how terrified? She, who had never left the area she had grown up in, despite her teenage dreams of ballroom dances and the promises of her husband before they married to take her to Paris, was about to embark on the greatest adventure of her life. She was about to go to Paris with the man she really loved, the man she had always loved.

The other passengers, assuming that Adele and Jules were husband and wife, minded their own business.

Adele took in the views streaming past her window, the distant snow-capped mountains she was leaving behind. Would she ever see them again? Would she miss them?

"We'll stop in Dijon after sunset," said Jules quietly. "There we will dine and sleep—and the horses will be replaced with fresh ones that will continue the journey early in the morning."

She had so many questions to ask, questions about his life over the past twenty years, about his previous visits to Paris, about what it would be like to live there with him. She had so many questions to ask but could not ask any of them in the crowded coach, and so she resumed staring out the window, pinching her arm gently to make sure this was not just another daydream.

"Don't worry, it will all be fine," he said quietly, as if reading her mind.

"When did you last take this trip?" she then whispered to him, still amazed that this humble man, this unpretentious schoolteacher who had not left her thoughts for the last two decades, had gotten himself in with such an important crowd and was used to travelling to Paris.

"The last time was a while ago, with Monsieur Voltaire, on his last trip to Paris in February 1778," he admitted. "He was eighty-four, but still insistent on taking the journey. I was one of his secretaries then, and he suspected that he might not return to Ferney. He told me as much."

Adele closed her eyes and listened to the rhythmic beat of the horses' hoofs. *Ta-tam, ta-tam, ta-tam.* Her body rocked with this rhythm and her heart finally slowed down; she thought that if it didn't, it might very well burst out of her chest.

She then felt her eyes closing and she wondered about leaning her head against Jules's shoulder. It was a strange feeling— the man next to her was at the same time a stranger, and her closest friend. She'd dreamed about him so often since she decided against marrying him, that sitting next to him on a carriage headed for Paris in real life seemed more of a fantasy than any of the daydreams she'd had over the past two decades.

In the end, her fatigue took over, as she'd barely closed her eyes the previous night. Her head dropped on Jules's shoulder and when the carriage stopped in Dijon a few hours later, he had to gently stroke her cheek to wake her up.

SIXTEEN

Geneva, 2018

We landed in Geneva mid-morning, and as we both just had carry-ons we quickly got in a taxi to Gex. Noah stared out the window the whole way, as he'd done for the past several hours on the plane.

"Say something," I said.

"I don't know what to say."

"Does any of this look familiar?" I asked.

"I've never been here before."

I sighed. Was this whole trip a waste of time, a fantasy that I've conjured up in my desperation to find a deeper meaning to life, as an answer to the turmoil and heartache I'd recently experienced? Was Noah just another random guy, someone I fell in love with briefly and then left—and then regretted having left him?

We got out of the taxi in Gex, and checked into two separate rooms I'd pre-booked at the Hotel Bellevue, the same small place I stayed at on my last visit to Gex. By the time I was in my room it was nearly midday, and I thought I'd have a shower and a rest before I met Noah for lunch at twelve-thirty, like we'd agreed.

To my dismay, when I woke up it was nearly three o'clock. I had missed my lunch appointment with Noah. What will he think now? He was upset with me anyway, probably more than just upset, since he didn't bother to bang on my door and wake me up.

I washed my face, brushed my teeth, and dressed quickly, and went to knock on Noah's door. There was no answer, and so I walked down the stairs to the small lobby, where the same

Frenchwoman who checked us in was adding up some numbers on a calculator.

"*Bonjour, madame*," she said.

"*Bonjour*," I said. "I am looking for my friend. I missed our lunch meeting, I overslept..."

"Oh, *le monsieur Américain*," she said. "He has gone some time ago. Maybe one o'clock?"

I looked at my watch again. So he was gone for over two hours.

"Did he say where he was going?" I asked. "Did he leave a message?"

"*Non, madame*," she said. "He did not leave a message. I am sorry."

"That's okay," I said, "*Merci beaucoup*. If he does come back, will you please tell him I went out looking for him, that I over-slept?"

"*Bien sûr, madame*," she said. "No problem."

I stepped out onto the bright afternoon. The street was al-most deserted, most of the shops still closed for their customary afternoon break. There was no one in sight. Where would I go? Where would I even start looking for him?

I walked the streets of Gex in the quiet afternoon, then it started clouding over. I passed the old church, with its beautiful lancet windows and pointed spire. I stopped by a little plaque, to read about the history of the church. It was built in the nine-teenth century and refurbished between 1954 and 1970, it said on the small brass sign. Did this church look familiar to me? Not really.

Perhaps I was losing my mind, like Don would have surely suggested had he been here with me, had he known what I was up to this afternoon?

I continued walking slowly up the street, and then stopped at a small *boulangerie* for a sandwich and a coffee. The shops were reopened now. It was nearly four o'clock, but I didn't know what else to do—and I just walked up the old alleys, looking for signs, for memories, looking for Noah. I didn't know where else to look, and so after nearly two hours of wandering the old streets of Gex aimlessly, I made my way back to the small main street, and to the Hotel Bellevue.

As I walked in, I saw him, sitting at the bar across from the lobby.

I went and sat on the barstool besides him.

"I'll have what he's having," I said to the barman.

"A double whiskey, *madame*?" asked the barman, slightly surprised. I guessed his average female customer did not order double whiskeys, certainly not before dark.

"Yes, a double whiskey, *s'il vous plaît*," I confirmed.

I looked at Noah, and he raised his eyebrows at me and took a long sip from his glass.

"You never drink," I said, my voice betraying my surprise.

"You're late for our lunch date," he said, but didn't sound angry.

"I am really sorry, I overslept. I didn't mean to..."

"It's okay," he said. "It gave me a chance to walk around a bit, and to think."

He looked as if he was going to say something more, and so I waited.

"It does all look oddly familiar," he finally said.

"Voila, *madame*," the barman put a glass in front of me. I stared at the ice cubes protruding from the amber-colored liquid. I then picked up the cold glass and emptied it in four large swigs, ignoring the disapproving look from the barman.

SEVENTEEN

Paris, 1789

They arrived in Paris just before sundown on Saturday. Some of the lanterns were already lit in the windows of houses they passed on their way into the city, and Adele felt exhilaration at the sight of the bridge they were about to cross, the *Pont Neuf*.

She had seen paintings and drawings of Paris, of course, and heard many stories about the glorious capital and its countless beauties and intrigues, but nothing could have prepared her for the setting of the late-May sunlight reflecting on the stones of the Pont Neuf. Connecting the two banks of the Seine, the bridge was like nothing she'd seen before. They rode into Paris from the south, and as the *grande diligence* slowed down and the horses moved into a gentle trot, she noticed other horses carrying well-dressed riders. They passed milkmaids, shoeshine boys and beggars dressed in rags, bare-chested men, barefooted children.

Adele was speechless, for she found no words to describe the joy mixed with dread that filled her chest. She had not imagined so many poor people existed on the streets of Paris—the dirty, ragged children, the filth, the misery. Where were those beautiful ballrooms she dreamed of all of her life? They must be there, somewhere. She suddenly felt like crying—crying not for herself, but for these scruffy looking men, women, and children they'd just passed.

Jules looked at her with his dark eyes and said nothing. He seemed unfazed by her astonishment with Paris. It had been part of her dreams and daydreams her entire life, and now it was he—not the man she chose over him twenty years back—who was helping make the dream of visiting Paris, a reality.

Then she caught him staring at her.

"What?" she asked.

He shook his head.

"Nothing."

"I can't believe we're here, together. I also can't believe that so many poor people live here on the streets…"

"We are here together," he said. "I just hope you won't regret leaving your old life and your family behind. Paris is very different from everything you know, everything you're accustomed to, in both good and bad ways. Presently, mostly in bad ways."

Adele took a deep breath, and as the carriage turned right from the Pont Neuf toward the Hotel de Ville and came to a halt, she knew for a fact that she would never go back to her old life. She would miss her family, no doubt. Her father, her mother, her children, perhaps even her brother Louis. Maybe even Pierre, for they had lived together for so many years. She would miss them, but she would not miss the dreary routine of the past thirty years. Now she knew exactly how a caged bird must feel when the door to its prison is opened and it is finally able to fly away. She had one man to thank for setting her free.

She took Jules extended hand and he helped her descend the carriage steps. She thanked the coachman; Jules tipped him. Adele looked up at the impressive municipality building and realized she had now put her fate and happiness in the hands of this man, who was presently negotiating with two scruffy looking youngsters who were offering to carry their cases to their lodgings.

The schoolteacher, used to dealing with youngsters—country and city dwellers alike—had reached an acceptable agreement and they now followed the two young men walking at a fast pace along the cobbled street.

"Where are we staying?" she asked and it occurred to her that she hadn't given this question a single thought since they left Gex the previous week.

"I've arranged rooms for us," said Jules, "in the home of Monsieur Jacob, a retired physician and old friend of Monsieur Voltaire's. We will settle here in the city. I have a few projects to tend to in the coming weeks, and I thought you might like the company of Madame Jacob. She is a very kind woman and makes interesting conversation."

Adele nodded. Only now the thoughts started racing in her mind—what will she do? How will she spend her time here in Paris? Reaching the city had been her lifelong dream since she had been a little girl, and now that the destination was reached she felt a bit out of sorts. *I could find work,* she thought. *I could teach children, I could write, I could help Jules with his proje*cts— those mysterious affairs he did not want to talk about, but were somehow related to Monsieur Voltaire and his friends. All it took was one look at the man walking with big, determined steps by her side to calm her anxiety and know that it would all be fine, one way or another.

EIGHTEEN

Gex, 2018

I suggested we call a taxi to take us to Chevry, instead of walking for twenty minutes along the main road as I had the previous time I was there. It was not a very pleasant walk, as there was no sidewalk, only short grass and cars driving past on a single-lane road.

"We can always walk back if we want to," I said, and Noah agreed.

"Can't you at least tell me why you are taking me there?" he asked, and I shook my head.

"Actually, no," I said.

"Is this some kind of test?"

"It is and it isn't," I said. "It's more of a test for me than for you. I'd really like to know if I am going mad, because I had such a powerful experience when I was there last time. But maybe it was just my imagination."

"Okay," he said. "I'll go with you on this one."

The receptionist called a taxi to take us to Chevry, and within minutes we were standing on the edge of the small village.

"Which way should we go?" I asked.

He looked at me.

"This is bizarre," he said. "Am I supposed to know this place? I am getting a feeling of déjà vu."

I got goose-bumps all over my arms and the back of my neck.

"Let's just walk," I said.

I let him lead the way, and as we walked around the small village I felt Noah relaxing, letting go of some of the palpable tension he'd held since he boarded the plane in New York.

We walked together as in a daydream, and when I put my hand in his he didn't pull away. We strolled along the small streets, past the church and up the Rue du Chateau. I tried not to lead Noah in any direction, but our feet walked as if they knew the way. As we approached the chateau, I hoped the gates would be open—as they happened to be the last time I was there—and I sighed in relief when I saw that they were. I couldn't restrain myself anymore.

"Let's go in," I said and pulled Noah by the hand.

"Are you sure?" he asked. "This looks like a private residence."

I nodded and stepped forward, but Noah didn't move.

"What's the matter?" I asked.

He was frozen to the spot.

"I know this place," he said.

"But you've never been here?" I asked, looking at him hopefully.

"I don't want to go in," he said. "This is creeping me out."

We stood there like two statues frozen in time; neither of us knowing what to do next.

"I am so sorry," he said.

"About what?" I asked. "I am the one who should be apologizing to you, if anything."

He shook his head.

"This place makes me feel dizzy. It makes me feel lost. It makes me feel... As if I've lost you."

"But you haven't lost me," I said. "I am right next to you."

He shook his head again.

"Let's go," he said. "I don't like this place, I don't like how it makes me feel."

I hesitated.

"We've come a long way for this, Noah."

He looked at me, and I noticed tears in his eyes.

He looked away.

"I don't want to lose you," he said.

NINETEEN

Paris, 1789

They'd been living in separate rooms for the past five days, and Adele was consumed with longing for Jules, even though he was near her most of the day. She did not know how or what to do with these feelings that completely overwhelmed her. He still acted as the responsible schoolteacher she knew from twenty years back, while she wanted him to be...she wanted him to be her lover now, not a responsible adult, with her longing for him like an irresponsible teenager.

Whether it was the fact she was married to someone else that acted as a deterrent, or whether he simply did not find her attractive anymore, she did not know, but she fully intended to find out.

She decided to sit and write a letter to her parents, although she knew they would probably return it unopened.

She could only imagine the turbulence her sudden departure had caused in their lives. How they might be shunned by the more pious neighbors, who made up more than half their village, and for whom adultery was a mortal sin. And yet, she hadn't even committed adultery—even though she had every hope of doing so soon. Indeed, she had left behind her husband, children, parents, her old life to live the kind of life she always wanted to live, a life of adventure in the big city. *I am no adulterer*, she thought. *I am an adventurer, like those I read about in novels.*

"*Chère maman, cher papa,*" she started writing, and then stopped. She hadn't written a letter in so many years, except for her short farewell notes. What could she tell them about her new life? She could imagine her mother sitting in the kitchen, her fingers hovering over the envelope. Will she decide to open it?

No, she must wait. They will calm down, everyone will calm down. Perhaps they'll eventually come to terms with her decision. Or maybe they will slowly forget that she was a part of their lives for so long. Her children may never forgive her, but the truth is that they were always more Pierre's children than her own. They loved their father. They put up with her, just like their grandparents—Pierre's parents—did.

She put the quill pen down and pushed the paper away. She'd write another day.

Her fears now emerged like the Horsemen of the Apocalypse, galloping through the exhilaration she first felt when they arrived the previous week. *Her family had no way of contacting her. What if something happened to her mother? Her father? Her children? What if she ended up on the streets of Paris, lonely and poor, like those people she saw when they first rode into the city?*

But she managed to push those thoughts aside for a little while. Now she had to concentrate on her Parisian life, on meeting people and perhaps even on helping Jules accomplish the mission he came to Paris for. She still knew no more about Jules's mysterious motives for coming to Paris, but she had her suspicions. Every afternoon around five o'clock, the curtains were drawn, the candles were lit and a small group would gather in the front room of their host, Monsieur Jacob. They were mostly men, although she had seen one or two women on one of the previous days. They would speak in hushed voices. Jules was the one taking notes and seemed to be moderating these meetings. Adele heard words such as "rebellion," "aristocracy," and "weapons" whispered, and sometimes even shouted and quickly hushed again.

She stayed in her room during those meetings; Jules preferred it that way. Then they would dine with Monsieur Jacob and his wife, once everyone had left.

"The less you are involved in these matters, the safer it is for you, my dear," said Jules. Despite calling her "my dear," *ma chérie*, they were not much more intimate than they'd been when they descended from the carriage the previous week in front of the Hotel de Ville. It was as if he was afraid to get too close to her, to touch her, to let his emotions loose.

He'd arranged for them to have separate rooms at Monsieur Jacob's house, and hers had a beautiful *poudreuse*, a dressing table with slender curved legs and a flowing design in rosewood and mahogany. It had four exterior drawers and a central mirror and she loved sitting in front of that mirror, on the beautiful matching chair with the bowed legs, listening to the voices coming from the front room.

She's never been into Jules's room but she had a glance at it when she passed by it in the corridor and the door was ajar—it was small and modest, not very different from a monastic cell. It was obvious that he had no need for luxury, no desire for earthly possessions. *How does he make a living?* she wondered. She decided to ask him at the first opportunity. First a schoolteacher, then one of Monsieur Voltaire's secretaries, and now also a qualified *maître d'armes*—a fencing master—these were the things she knew about him. And yet it seemed to her that the more details she learned about Jules Badeau's life, the more mysterious he became to her.

When she tried to touch his hand, his shoulder, his face, he didn't pull back. But he never initiated any close contact and even though it has been less than a week since they arrived in Paris, she was starting to wonder if they would ever get physically close. *Should she try to go into his room*, she wondered. *Should she ask him about it?* Having a dream of so many years become reality was confusing—as if the dreams of the past became her present reality, and her past was a distant dream.

As soon as the voices stopped and the group of people left Monsieur Jacob's home, Adele brushed her hair, applied some fresh *rouge* on her cheeks, and after turning left and right in front of the mirror to make sure everything looked good, she left to join Jules in the front room.

She found him with Monsieur Jacob, both holding glasses of wine—Jules's was full, Monsieur Jacob's was empty—and exchanging words in hushed voices.

"Ah, Adele," exclaimed Monsieur Jacob. "I am so sorry, our meeting took longer than usual this afternoon. I hope you are not getting bored."

"I would be getting much less bored if I was allowed to attend," said Adele in a voice that tried to convey lightheartedness but failed. Monsieur Jacob and Jules exchanged glances.

"*Ma chérie*," said Jules, "why don't we go for a walk along the Seine after we dine with Monsieur and Madame Jacob?"

"Of course," said Adele, "that would be wonderful."

And so, after a modest dinner with the elderly couple, they went out into the warm Parisian evening, Adele's arm linked in Jules's.

"It is a sad day for me today," he admitted. "Exactly eleven years ago Monsieur Voltaire died, here in Paris. I was outside his room when he died, and helped with the formalities after his death, as did Monsieur Jacob. He truly changed my life. Without him I would be a nobody."

"You would have never been a nobody," said Adele. "You were always someone. In fact, I think you always were a greater man than most men I know."

Jules did not reply.

Adele decided to change the subject.

"Jules," she started, hesitant at first. "Could you tell me more about these meetings. Why are they such a secret? I would so like to be a part of your life now, after all these years. I would like to be a part of your life...in everything."

He gave her a sideways glance, and she felt herself blushing.

Jules continued walking silently, considering his answer.

"*Ma chérie,*" he started, "great things are happening now in Paris, great things that will influence our glorious country. But they are dangerous things too. If we succeed, we will be rewarded. The people of France will be rewarded, for they shall have power and will no longer suffer at the hands of the aristocracy. This is something that Monsieur Voltaire was strongly in favor of, but he is no longer around to assist us. However, many of us gave our word to him that we will continue his work. It is important work, and we will be victorious in the end, but if we were to fail…well if we failed, who knows what would happen to the people of France. I am worried about getting you involved in such matters."

"But I can help!" exclaimed Adele. "I am no longer eighteen, you know. I can help you, and your friends. Whatever the cause of Monsieur Voltaire, and your cause, it is my cause too now. And Jules…" she hesitated, but then stopped and reached up for his cheek.

Jules turned to her, and looked into her eyes for a few moments, which seemed to her like an eternity.

"Very well, *ma chérie*," he finally said. He gently lifted her chin and their lips touched tenderly at first, and then more passionately, as the longing that they had held between them for the past twenty years melted into an all-consuming kiss.

TWENTY

Chevry, 2018

I took Noah's hand and pulled him through the gates of the Chateau de Chevry. He did not object. In fact, it was as if he was sleepwalking, the expression on his face at once dreamy and fearful.

We first wandered around the chateau's garden, then entered through the building's gate, and into the main hall where paintings and portraits were displayed and the stone walls held two-hundred-year-old secrets I was determined to expose.

Noah let go of my hand and walked alone, his shoulders suddenly hunched, his step careful and hesitant.

It pained me to see him like that. It was as if I was watching him time travel, metamorphosing into an old man, full of regrets. My heart was heavy with something resembling grief, something that I could not explain even to myself.

I took his hand again and led him to the collection of ancient swords hanging on the far wall, above the open fireplace, and we stood underneath them together, looking up.

He read the plaque that said, *En memoire de Jules Badeau, enseignant et maître d'armes, 1745–1807* and looked at me in wonder.

"What?" I said.

He shrugged and covered his face with his hands.

I stood silently by his side. We must have stood there together for a good five minutes before the same elderly lady I met last time walked in.

"*Bonjour, madame et monsieur,*" she said.

"*Bonjour, madame,*" I answered.

I felt Noah's hand squeezing my arm just a little too hard.

I decided to take the risk, despite my French being a bit rusty.

"Excuse me, *madame*," I said. "My friend here is trying to find some information about an ancestor. I see his name on the plaque here. It's Monsieur Jules Badeau."

The woman looked at me, then at the plaque, then at Noah.

"Perhaps we have some old documents, that are not on display," she said hesitantly.

"But I am not sure if I can take them out, let me ask my husband, *le guardian*. There might also be a portrait of the Master, with the children he taught. I remember seeing it in the storage room a while back when I cleaned in there."

She shuffled to the exit and Noah and I waited there, speechless. Time stood still, but when she returned ten minutes later, carrying something in her hands, I felt a pain in my stomach. What had she brought back?

"I am sorry," she said. "I am not allowed to take any documents out of storage, they are all carefully put away. But I found this."

She unwrapped a piece of soft white fabric and produced a medium-sized portrait, in dark watercolors. It showed an elderly man with sad eyes, standing beside three boys dressed in old-style white breeches and jackets, the youths proudly displaying their fencing swords. All three boys had fair wavy hair and large brown eyes. The man looked like an older version of Noah.

TWENTY-ONE

West Africa, 1577

He lived in the shaman's hut. Many moons had passed since the ghost-men came and brutally took the life of his teacher, as well as the lives of many other young men. *They also took some with them*, said one of the older women. She had hid in the forest, close to the village, and saw them drag the chained young men, forcing them into the boats that then disappeared down the river. There were no crocodiles waiting for them this time, for she heard no screams of men being eaten alive.

In no time they disappeared from view, said the elderly woman, tears rolling down her cheeks.

They left behind them only charred earth and a strange weapon, which the woman now handed to the apprentice.

"One of the ghost-men put it down and then left it behind when they got into the boat," she said to him. She, despite her age and her fear, had snuck down to the riverbank and recovered it. Not for herself, of course, she now said. Perhaps it could be of use to the young apprentice, for it seemed to have magical powers. She'd never seen anything like it.

It was a kind of short spear with an elaborate handle that looked like an ancient sea creature with many arms, hard but sleek to the touch. It ended with a sharp tip, which the apprentice now carefully examined. It was longer than his arm, and quite heavy. It was certainly a magical weapon, but it did not seem like one of those that can kill from afar, it was perhaps meant for stabbing or slashing—the apprentice did not know, for he was not a warrior.

He thanked the old woman for retrieving it, and said he

would ask the forefathers' spirits to remove the dark magic from this thing.

The apprentice took the strange object back with him, and after examining it, he buried it in the ground not far from his hut. He wanted to keep it somewhere where it could do no harm, until he could figure out what to do with it.

He now felt the burden of comforting others, who came to him for they had no one else to go to.

His mother took over the practical arrangements, despite her natural shyness that stemmed from the fact she was deaf-mute, unable to hear or speak. She made sure those who came to seek her son's advice did so in an orderly manner, and that he had plenty of time to rest, and food to eat.

It was a strange experience, almost as if reality had shifted, leaving him in charge of things—him, a fresh-faced young man, collecting plants and herbs at dusk, and drying them, grinding them and then administering them to those who came to him with illnesses, with questions, with requests, with a tremor in their voices.

He continued to feel the presence of his mentor, the old shaman, all around him. Living in the old man's hut, surrounded by his few earthly possessions—and some that seemed unearthly— was like living under his constant guidance.

Now that you live in your own hut, said his mother in her odd sign language, which only he could decipher, *perhaps you need a wife.*

Of all the village girls—there were plenty of them around, and very few young men—he had always liked one. Tall and slim, her dark skin smooth and beautiful, her long hair braided into small, delicate sections. She was called Mukambu. But he had never exchanged any words with her, merely shy glances. He didn't think he was good enough for her—but before, he was only an apprentice boy. Now he was the village's medicine man, even if his talents were yet to be proven. And all those young men, all the warriors who were the fiercest and the bravest and the most charming, all of them...now gone. Some had gone to the Other Side, others had gone with the ghost-men, in chains, to another Other Side, unknown to them. There was only him left, him and some younger boys who were not yet fit for marriage. So perhaps... Perhaps he stood a chance with Mukambu now.

Mukambu came to see him, together with her mother and her younger sister. Her younger sister, Oputu, was burning with fever. *She has been ill for a few days now,* said her mother. *None of the usual herbs and roots worked, what were they to do now,* she asked. *Was it perhaps a curse?*

He held the girl's wrist, and immediately noticed something was wrong. Her life force was irregular, like a drumbeat with a half-beat missing. He was not sure what to do, but he closed his eyes and focused, asking for help. First, all he could see was mist. Soon, the mist started clearing, and he felt the Life Force coming through him, from the top of his head and into his torso and then his arms and hands, onto the little girl. He held her, and she sat like a soft ball of moss in his arms until, after some time had passed—she turned solid again. He remembered the way the shaman used to rock backward and forward to a melody he alone could hear in his head—but now he, his apprentice, could hear that same melody. It was soft and divine, it was a hum and it was a song and it was the sound of the universe.

And then it stopped and the little girl was fast asleep in his arms. He handed her back to her mother and noticed that her sister, the beautiful Mukambu, was looking at him with something resembling admiration. He felt his hands tremble and was not sure whether it was because of the way she had just looked at him or because of the Life Force that had passed through his hands and into another being, something that he had never felt before—not quite like this. He knew that the old shaman used to

do this regularly—he'd watched him do it many, many times—
but he was always a passive observer, never an active healer
himself. Until now.

TWENTY-TWO

Paris, 1789

The streets of Paris were filled with excitement, with change bubbling under the surface; Adele could feel it as soon as she ventured out. The few flowers along the Seine quickly withered in the July heat, and she was no longer troubled at night by the thoughts about the family she had left behind. The purpose she felt in her previous life as a mother and wife was now replaced by a newfound purpose: a revolutionary, or *une petite révolutionnaire* as Monsieur Jacob liked to call her since she started attending their meetings. Her endless moments of staring blankly at her embroidery seemed as if they were in a different lifetime, a lifetime she did not want to go back to. Yes, she missed her children—but she knew beyond doubt that they were well taken care of. In fact, she thought, they are probably better off without her. Her mother-in-law would have taken charge by now, turning their minds against her.

"Your good-for-nothing *maman* has abandoned you," she could hear Madame Bertrand's voice in her mind as she walked along the Seine, toward the Pont Neuf. The carriages that crossed the bridge hovered in front of her eyes as if they were images in a dream. She passed a group of fish-sellers, ladies with broad faces and wild hair. They looked at her suspiciously as she walked past them. She could still remember how impressed she was when Pierre Bertrand—she had difficulties calling him "husband" even in her mind now—wore a stock with a black *solitaire*, which was the fashion in Paris nearly two decades ago. He imported fabrics and the latest Parisian fashion to the small town of Gex, a place full of farmers. *Les paysans,* she remembered her mother-in-law's voice, full of contempt when she used to speak of the local farmers.

"What do they understand? What do they know about fashion?" she used to say to her sons, who ran the family shop, "It is like casting pearls before swine."

She was sure that Madame Bertrand never forgave Pierre for having married a *paysan*'s daughter. *Now she'll be happy to have been proven right,* thought Adele.

The clouds above her floated calmly and she shaded her eyes with her hand as she looked at them. A sudden commotion made her turn, as someone grabbed her arm and pushed her to the ground.

Her eyes at the height of the carriage wheels, her beautiful green dress in the dirt, she was about to protest when she heard a gunshot, and saw a man running off the bridge, heading east. She did not get a clear view of the man from her position on the ground. But she did notice his brown boots, long white socks, and black breeches as he ran into the distance.

Shouting and neighing followed as one of the horses tried to rear up on its back legs, causing the other horse to pull back, and the carriage to almost turn over.

A man's hand was extended to her and she let him pull her onto her feet.

"*Desolé, madame,*" he said, tipping his hat. "*Vous allez bien?*"

"Yes," she said, "I'm fine, thank you."

"These revolutionaries are getting worse by the day," said the gentleman. "They think they own Paris now, but they will get their justice, don't you worry."

"Revolutionaries?" she asked, and the man nodded.

"Excuse me, *madame*, someone got shot."

He left her side and made his way to the beautifully ornate yellow carriage. Another gentleman was holding the well-groomed horses by the harness and the coachman was nowhere to be seen.

She carefully approached the carriage, curious to see more, but she was pushed back by a throng of people moving away.

"The King's Guards are arriving!" she heard someone shout, and everyone started running off the bridge. She followed, carried along with the escaping throng.

She wanted to understand more, she wanted to know what had happened—but the sound of dozens of hooves galloping toward the bridge from the west convinced her that perhaps this was not the moment to stay around and ask questions. She would ask Jules; she was certain he would be able to explain things to her. And so she headed back to Monsieur Jacob's house.

Adele arrived at the building on Rue de Buci breathless. It took her ten minutes to run from the Pont Neuf to Monsieur Jacob's residence, her feet carrying her like wings. Her mind was full of questions, she heard things whispered in the streets now— revolution, liberty, equality. Down with the aristocracy, down with the church. She wanted to know more, and she knew that these ideas had a greater meaning, perhaps this was what Jules was referring to when he talked of his debt to Monsieur Voltaire. These ideas, they were the "transparent truth," as she'd heard Jules refer to them. Jules, her darling Jules, who was willing to sacrifice his own life and happiness for the cause of the revolution, as he'd told her himself the day before.

They were walking together in the evening toward the Pont Neuf, just like she'd done alone earlier today. She leaned on him as the Parisian evening breeze caressed her hair and she knew she'd made the right decision to come to Paris.

It was not a decision anyone back home would understand, or accept, or ever forgive her for—that she was quite certain of. But it was a decision that made her feel alive, as if she'd finally connected to her life's purpose, even if she'd done that twenty years too late.

And no, perhaps it was not twenty years too late, she thought. *Perhaps it was the right thing to marry Pierre Bertrand, and to have his children, for she loved her children very much and knew they'd grow up to be good young people.*

Jules, her wonderful Jules, was probably not made for marriage and children—some men are just like that, they serve a greater purpose than that of most men. Had she stayed with him perhaps he would have been trapped in a small town struggling to provide for a family; living an ordinary life. But he was not meant to live an ordinary life, he was meant to change the world, and certainly could not do that from a small town near the Swiss border. His place was in Paris, in this bustling city among artists and revolutionaries, and her place was by his side.

And so she arrived at Monsieur Jacob's house, ready to tell Jules about the event on the bridge. As she entered the front room she was greeted by hushed whispers of four men huddled together in the corner.

Jules turned to her.

"Ah, Adele, you're back."

He walked toward her and put his hand on the small of her back, leading her out of the room.

"Jules, *mon chéri,* you won't believe what just happened on the Pont Neuf, someone got shot in plain daylight! A man arrived and…"

Jules put his hand over her lips. His face was serious, almost grim.

"Adele, hush."

"What is the matter?"

He pointed behind him, in the direction of the front room.

"We have a visitor. He will be staying here during the day, but when night falls I will have to accompany him to the countryside."

"Oh, Jules… What do you mean, are you going away?"

"Just for a few days, *ma chérie.* Just a few days. There are serious things happening. We need to protect our rights, our freedom. You will be safe here with Monsieur and Madame Jacob…

but if anyone comes to inquire, you mustn't say anything."

"What do you mean? Who would come to inquire…?"

"You mustn't say anything about the man, or about my going to the countryside with him. Do you understand? This is very important."

"Yes, yes, I understand, but…but why? Why did someone on the bridge shoot an innocent man? Those people in the carriage did not provoke him…he just shot them!"

Jules hesitated.

"The less you know about this, the better, Adele. But the man in the carriage was not an innocent man. He was the treasurer of the King, stealing food from the people of the *patrie*, of the nation. We are a nation of free men and women, *ma chérie*, but the people are hungry for bread. They have nothing. You must know this already, of course. No one can get in the way of that freedom. Especially not the King's men."

They stared at each other silently, then Adele fell into Jules's arms, and they stood there together for several moments. She could feel his heartbeat, his warm chest.

He finally pushed her back gently.

"Adele, I will be back as soon as I can. I do not want to be away from you anymore. I have waited for this for long enough. So many years," he said.

"Oh, Jules," she said, her eyes filling with tears. "My darling Jules. I will miss you so much. We have never even…"

He looked down at her, and smiled.

"We will, Adele, we will. I want us to feel comfortable with each other first. This is not why I took you from your family, all the way to Paris. It is not for the carnal pleasures that I want you to be with me here."

They didn't go out for the rest of the day, and kept the curtains drawn. She dined with Monsieur and Madame Jacob, and Jules, later that evening. There was no sign of the stranger in the house, although she could hear someone clearing their throat in one of the rooms down the corridor, and a plate of food was taken in there.

As Jules was preparing to leave just after it got dark—at around ten thirty that evening—she finally caught a glimpse of the stranger. All she could see was his back, but she couldn't help but notice the brown boots and black breeches as he quietly walked out of the door together with Jules into the warm early July night.

TWENTY-THREE

Gex, 2018

We didn't speak on our walk back to Gex. Noah was in a dark mood, as if the afternoon's events burdened him greatly. After the *guardian*'s wife showed us the painting he mumbled a few words of thanks and pulled me out of there, not even giving me the opportunity to explain anything to the surprised lady; to find some excuse for our abrupt and ungrateful departure.

I couldn't speak even if I wanted to; my voice would not obey me. I wanted to ask him what he thought, how he felt about what he saw and experienced just moments earlier, but the determination in which he walked toward Gex and his brooding expression were enough to deter me from even trying.

We got back to our hotel in Gex after a brisk twenty-minute walk, and I felt emotionally drained. There was nothing I could say or do; my mind was blank.

Noah headed straight to his room, without saying a word, and I headed to mine.

Was it all a big mistake, a huge waste of time? Traveling from New York all the way to France to chase an imaginary experience, something I could not explain even to myself, something that probably did not exist at all?

I wasn't hungry, I wasn't sad, I wasn't even curious anymore. I was just tired, so tired that I kicked my sandals off, lay on the bed fully dressed, and fell asleep without even pulling the covers over me.

And, after many long weeks of absence, that's when the shaman's apprentice came to tell me his story.

The apprentice decided to experiment. Not on people at first, but on himself. All those years he'd spent watching the shaman, learning from him, basking in the warmth and confidence that his energy had instilled—all those years had stayed with him. But they were not enough, nowhere near enough. They were like early-morning fog in the forest, with its brown and orange trees, inviting, tempting, promising. And then gone—gone, gone, just like his beloved mentor.

It was no coincidence that such holy duties were passed down from father to son, he thought, *but the old man did not have a son, and he did not have a father.* And so, the shaman had treated him like a son after he saved his life when he was an infant. He considered the old man the closest thing to a father that he'd ever known, for he did not know his real father. In fact, he had no idea who his real father was. His mother never said—not that she could say anything in words—but she knew very well what he wanted to know, as he'd asked several times before he decided to stop.

Where is my father? he'd ask her, and she pretended not to understand the question, although she understood everything else he'd ever tried to convey to her in signs.

But she would not say, and after a while it didn't matter anymore. His mentor became his father, and that was enough. He taught him to recognize medicinal plants, to dry and grind them into powder, which he then packed into small leather sachets. He taught him to recognize the paw prints of different animals, and also the prints of their souls. He taught him to connect to their spirits and ask for their help when he needed it, and he taught him to help every living being, even if he needed to take its life away for some reason. The animals that served as vehicles of the divine force—such as snakes, deer, birds, even monkeys—did so in mutual agreement. The animal energy that he was taught to harness was not wild, was not random. It had a purpose; it served something greater than him, greater than them all.

He had learned all these things from his mentor, from the

old medicine man, but now that he was gone—murdered by the cruel ghost-people—everything he had taught him seemed to have transformed to misty memories. Now he was on his own, and people were counting on him to help them. He had to find a way, and perhaps the way was to experiment—to find his own path and channel to the souls of the people he was trying to help, to the spirits of the animals, and most important—to those of the forefathers.

He started by venturing into the forest during the day. There he conversed with the trees, with the birds, with the small animals whose paw prints he'd encountered, with the larger animals that watched him suspiciously from their hideaways.

You have to earn their trust, his mentor had told him many moons ago, but he didn't tell him how that trust was to be earned.

He left small gifts for the monkeys, and they started following him in the forest, jumping from branch to branch high above his head. They could find their own fruit, of course, for the forest was lush with nourishment, with gifts of nature. But leaving them small presents seemed to have a special significance—it helped create a bond.

We are the protectors of nature, said the old shaman.

Why would nature need our protection, he had wondered back then, but now he was beginning to understand. Nature was immense, strong, and fierce—but it was also fragile, delicate, in need of chaperones. He began to see that the relationship between all living things was complex and interwoven. One thing affected another; it was all part of a living, breathing fabric that was connected in ways he could not always understand, but he was determined to learn more about. He wanted to understand it more than anything, and deeply regretted not having asked his mentor more questions when he could have. But perhaps he still could, even now?

The shaman had spoken about connecting with the forefathers, and now he himself had turned into one of the forefathers, as he had passed to the Other Side.

He decided to try to connect directly with his mentor. There was that *special place*, the place where the old man used to go to and spend the night on occasions, when he needed to have an important consultation with the forefathers. He went there before he was slaughtered by the pale-faced men, but he never told his apprentice where this place was.

We each find the place where we can make the connection, he said to the young man once. *We find it and then we make it ours, we imprint our energy there, although we never really own it,* he added.

Now the young apprentice was determined to find his mentor's special place, just to see what he could feel there. Yes, he will also need to have a place of his own where he can connect to the forefathers, but now he wanted — more than anything — he wanted to find a place where he could connect to his mentor.

The shaman was buried in the forest, not far from the graves of his ancestors. Three large birds, their wings the span of old beech wood tree branches, stood by his grave as if protecting it.

"They are guarding it from evil spirits," said the apprentice to himself.

He visited the grave daily at first, and then weekly. He would go to the outskirts of the village at sundown, to sit by his teacher's grave and talk to him, ask questions.

He would not always hear the answers but more often than not, they would be there — clear in his mind.

The apprentice knew that the shaman was not really gone; he was just different now.

One evening, he decided to spend the night by his teacher's grave, to see if he could learn something more, if the old man would come to him in his dreams.

He knew that the dreams opened the door to another state of consciousness, another reality that was just as real as the one he could touch and feel with his other senses.

And so he lit a small fire and sat chanting through the night, his shoulders covered with the shaman's old cape. It smelled of earth and fire and medicinal herbs.

When the moon was high above the trees and the only sounds that could be heard in the forest were some frogs and nocturnal insects hunting for prey, the apprentice stopped chanting. He fell asleep, and he dreamed.

In his dream, the shaman held a stick, not any kind of plain stick, but one made of something shiny and hard, with a sharp edge. The apprentice recognized it immediately. It was the object the old woman had given him; the object the ghost-men left behind.

The shaman waved this strange stick around in sweeping motions and was trying to tell him something but the apprentice could not hear the words. He could only see the shaman's lips moving and the motions of his hand holding the haunted object.

He tried to ask his teacher why he was waving this shiny stick around, why was he making strange stabbing motions. Did the stick have magic powers?

The apprentice tried to touch the image but it was too elusive to touch.

He awoke from his dream to a strange noise, the wings of a bird. He could remember the details of his dream vividly; it was still there behind his closed eyelids. When he opened his eyes, just before the crack of dawn, there were the three birds standing by the shaman's grave. Three large, dark birds, before dawn in the jungle. He did not know what kind of birds these were, nor did he care. He knew that in reality they were not birds, but spirits, sent from the Other Side to tell him something, to deliver a message.

I awoke with a start. I also thought I could hear the flutter of wings, but when I opened my eyes and looked around me there was nothing. There was just quiet darkness in the very room in which I fell asleep, in the small hotel in Gex, France.

I sat upright, confused by this dream within a dream. What did it mean?

I realized I was still fully dressed, and got up slowly to wash my face.

It is early, but maybe I'll get undressed and shower.

But then I had another idea.

I pulled my laptop out of my small suitcase, where it had sat since I packed it back home, just in case I could get some work done.

But instead of pulling up a manuscript to edit, I clicked on the file I had started a while back. The file titled "Premonitions."

And I started typing, my fingers doing the work all by themselves.

TWENTY-FOUR

Paris, 1789

The following week Jules offered to take Adele to a fencing *salle*, the same one he had frequented during his previous *sejours* in Paris.

Adele could not stop looking at Jules's profile as he walked by her side, thinking she would never get enough of looking at him, after all these years of dreaming *of* looking at him.

"In the sixteenth century Charles IX gave the *maîtres d'armes*, the fencing masters in Paris, special treatment," Jules said as they walked toward the *salle*. "The subsequent kings extended the royal privilege."

"What does that mean?"

"It means that they had royal favoritism. In 1643 Louis XIV emphasized that fencing masters should not only be experienced in feats of arms but they should be well born, have manners, and be skilled in conversation. And some fifteen years later, he created the Academy of Fencing."

They eventually turned the corner. Jules pointed to an elaborately engraved symbol above a heavy wooden door.

"This is the symbol of the *Académie d'armes de France*," he said.

She looked at the crossed swords under a mask and royal shield, and smiled at Jules.

"So you learned to fence here?"

"Monsieur Voltaire made the introductions for me some years back," he said. "Although when I lived in Lyon and trained as a teacher I did try to fence a little, so it was not completely new to me. When I was young I neither believed in violence nor had the means to pay for the lessons."

"And now you believe in violence?" she asked.

He didn't answer at first.

"When one is young, one tends to see the world in black and white, tends to be for or against things. As one grows older, one sees that there are many shades of right and wrong. Nothing is absolute."

"And what about killing a man?"

"When it is in protection of oneself or of the *patrie*, perhaps," he said quietly.

Adele considered his words.

"The man you took to the countryside," she said. "He killed a man."

Jules's face darkened.

"You mustn't mention him to anyone," he said. "Ever."

Adele nodded.

Jules opened the door and held it for Adele, as they walked into the *salle*. Adele stood in the corner while Jules greeted some of the men.

She watched as the Master, a thin, elegant man with a dark mustache corrected some of the student fencers. Jules picked up a sword and showed it to her.

"This is a *fleuret*, a practice and training weapon. See? There is a leather button to blunt it, and it looks like a flower bud, doesn't it? That's why we call it a *fleuret*, flower blossom."

The *maître d'armes* then approached them and shook Jules hand.

"Welcome, *bienvenue*," he said.

Jules introduced them.

"This is the best fencing master in Paris," he said, his hand on the *maître d'armes* shoulder. "He was a good friend of the late Monsieur Voltaire," he added.

The man nodded.

"And any friend of Monsieur Voltaire's is a friend of mine," he said to Jules.

"You see," said Jules, "this is where anyone who wants to become a good fencer comes to train. For three livres a month, a man can come and practice the art of fencing and learn from the best."

The fencing master brushed his mustache with two fingers.

"Unless, you'd like a private lesson, *madame*, in which case I will charge you only two livres."

Adele laughed.

"Me, fencing? What an idea," she said.

"I don't see why not," said Jules. "I believe women could be as good fencers as men."

It was the *maître d'armes'* turn to laugh now.

"What interesting ideas you have, Monsieur Badeau," he said.

Adele walked around the *salle* and looked at the display of swords, fencing masks, and fencing jackets. She observed the men in training, while Jules and the fencing master had a quiet exchange in the corner.

As they left the *salle*, Jules seemed pleased.

"I've entered into an agreement with this master. I've known him for many years. He agreed to work with me further, so one day perhaps I can teach fencing together with him, and assist him. It is an advantage that I fence left-handed, but of course do practice right-hand fencing, too. A *maître d'armes* should be able to fence with both hands."

"Teach with him, at his club?" Adele asked, with a hint of surprise.

"Not everyone can teach fencing here in Paris," said Jules. "One needs to be well born to be accepted as a *maître* here, but perhaps one day if we go back to…"

He stopped midsentence when he saw the look on Adele's face.

"We can never go back," she said. "*I* can never go back."

"I am sorry," he said, and took her hand and kissed it. Adele, who was not used to such small and tender displays of affection, felt her eyes stinging.

As they strolled back along the Seine, Jules told her that it was the eleventh anniversary of Jean-Jacques Rousseau's death.

"It pains me that another great Frenchman will not get to see the fruits of his hard work," he said sadly. "I met him once when I accompanied Monsieur Voltaire to Geneva. The two men disliked each other, but I liked them both. They never seemed to agree on anything. Such different temperaments. But you must read Rousseau's writings, *ma chérie*. Start with *The Social Contract*."

"What is it about?" she asked.

"Monsieur Voltaire referred to Rousseau's *The Social Contract* as 'a book against the human race' but I disagree. In the time Monsieur Voltaire spent in England 'where men and minds were free,' as he used to say, he wrote, *Letters on the English*. Monsieur Rousseau had admitted that this book had a great influence on him—but Voltaire was too proud to return the kindness when it came to Monsieur Rousseau's work. He also called Rousseau's beautiful romance *Julie, or the New Heloise,* 'a silly book' but I would recommend that you read that one too, if you haven't already."

He stopped and chuckled, before he added, "Even if Monsieur Voltaire speculated that half of it was written in a brothel and the second half in the lunatic asylum. But I truly think he said that out of jealousy. These two couldn't exist without each other. They even died only one month apart. If there is a heaven, they are surely sitting there together now, still arguing with each other."

A man who recommends which books she should read; who jokes with her; who understands her interest in intellectual matters; who considers her an equal and speaks to her as an equal!

Adele was more enamored than ever.

"Jules, I am so happy I came with you to Paris," she said.

"Even if it means that I can never go back."

He stopped again and looked at her, his dark eyes concerned.

"You genuinely have no regrets about leaving your family?" he asked.

"I truly feel like the most fortunate woman in the world to be with you here, Jules. I've never felt like this before, and if I die tomorrow, I will die a happy woman."

"I am sorry it took me so long," he said. "All this missed time. But had I asked you to marry me back then...would you have married me?"

She hesitated just a moment too long before answering.

"Probably," she said.

"No, you wouldn't have," he stated. "I was just a school-teacher. Your family wanted you to marry Pierre Bertrand. I can understand that."

She didn't know what to say, and so did not contradict his statement.

"But," he then said, "this is how life works. When the timing is right, things happen. If it is not right, they don't. So there's no real use for regrets."

Adele nodded silently, secretly wiping a tear off her cheek.

Jules glanced at her sideways, not quite sure how to stop her from being sad.

"Every gentleman should train in fencing, dancing, and horsemanship," he then said, changing the subject. "I was for-tunate to be able to train in these gentlemanly arts thanks to Monsieur Voltaire. I would have been a different man today had I not worked for him and had he not taken a liking to our con-versations. And so he decided to help and further my training."

"I don't know anyone who fences," said Adele. "Not many people do in our parts."

"Of course, where we come from there is no school of fenc-ing. I was hoping to change that," said Jules. "But now...we will see."

"Why is fencing so important, anyway?" she asked. "I can understand horsemanship. I can certainly understand dancing."

"Fencing is for honorable men, for it is all about honor," said Jules. "It is about facing your rival with dignity, and adhering to a code, even if you end up disarming, or even killing, your opponent. It is an art and an obligatory skill for any gentleman of good character and good breeding. Those who are of shady character will just drag one out and try to beat them up in a dark alley. There's no honor in that, is there?"

"But what is it that made it so important to Monsieur Voltaire, and to you?"

Jules reflected on her question.

"When Monsieur Voltaire was young, he thought swordsmanship to be a man's last resort, he always preferred the pen, his *plume*," he said. "Then, when he was in his early thirties he had a falling-out with a powerful nobleman, the Chevalier de Rohan. Monsieur Voltaire used his best tool against him—this was his writing, of course—but the nobleman paid some lowly people to beat Monsieur Voltaire up. It created a big scandal and was obviously a cowardly thing to do. But Monsieur Voltaire, seeking to defend his own honor, challenged this nobleman to a duel. However, on the morning of the duel he was arrested!"

Adele opened her eyes wide.

"Why?" she asked.

"Guy Auguste de Rohan-Chabot, the Chevalier de Rohan, was the son of the Duc of Rohan and the Marquise de Vardes. A very powerful noble family," said Jules. "They obtained a *lettre de cachet*—a direct order from the King—and got Monsieur Voltaire thrown into the Bastille prison. He was then given two options: a prison term, or exile to England."

"I know which one he chose, of course," said Adele. "Everyone knows."

"Indeed," said Jules. "And a wise choice as well, because the ideas that he was exposed to in *Angleterre* helped make him the inspiring man he became."

"It is interesting that he still thought fencing an important skill for a gentleman, even though it got him into prison," said Adele.

Jules stopped and looked at her.

"As for me," he said quietly, "I was never good at expressing my feelings in words. I always had to put on a facade—as a teacher, and as a man. But when I put the fencing mask on..." he paused. Adele waited for him to continue. She noticed for the first time how the burning streetlamps created a yellow light around them and felt grateful, grateful to be standing next to Jules on the streets of Paris, and listening to his melodic voice telling her about...about who he really was.

"When I put the fencing mask on, I feel I can be who I really am," he said. "No one watches my expression, no one can see how I really feel. I can smile, I can cry, I can be myself, as the mask not only protects my face from possible blows, but protects my emotions, in a strange way. I am not making much sense, am I?"

Adele smiled at him.

"You are true to yourself under the mask," she said.

He nodded.

"Whatever the future may bring, Adele," he said, "My heart is full now."

"Why do you say such a thing?" she asked. "It sounds ominous."

"It does," he said. "Perhaps it is just my cautious nature, perhaps a premonition. Only time will tell. But I have to go away again next week, for a couple of weeks this time."

Adele moved closer to him and he put his arms around her. They stood together, for the whole world to see how close they felt. They watched the ripples on the Seine, happy to be together before life's turmoil tore them apart again.

TWENTY-FIVE

Gex, 2018

I stopped typing as the first rays of sunlight streamed through a gap in the curtains.

It has been so long since I've given the shaman and his apprentice any thought, that I've almost forgotten about them. Now I could smell them in the room—the deep, earthy odor of African soil after the rain. The fear, the isolation, the desperation the shaman must have felt in his last moments. And the hope that his apprentice carried with him.

Maybe it wasn't for nothing. Maybe I am supposed to understand something through this dream, through this whole trip to France. Maybe if I dare, I can even talk to Noah about it; he is only a short distance away. But Noah didn't want to talk—it was quite obvious from his behavior last night, from his conduct over the past few weeks. He just retreated into his shell and stayed there, protecting himself from any attempt I made to get him to open up to me. And who could blame him?

I rejected him shortly after our love affair started. I went back to the arrogant, self-assured Don, who betrayed me and the life we had worked so hard to build for our children.

And Noah, whose social skills were lacking and seemingly only able to show the beauty of his soul to his students, was left out in the cold.

I stood up and washed my face, then pulled a cardigan around my shoulders. I tiptoed out of my room. It was just after six in the morning; in a desperate attempt to find comfort, I decided I would go and see Noah straight away and take my chances. What's the worst that could happen?

The carpet in the corridor was soft under my bare feet, and I took the stairs down. Noah's room was on the floor below mine—I was on the second floor; he was on the first.

I approached his door with trepidation, still hesitating whether it was a good idea to knock on it so early in the morning. Would he understand why I'd come to him? Was there enough trust between us to allow such a move on my part? I hoped there was.

I hoped he'd see beyond what seemed like an intrusion, a carnal temptation, or something in-between, for in reality it was something much deeper, something I could not put into words.

I knocked quietly, once.

The door opened slowly, and Noah looked at me without a hint of surprise.

"I couldn't sleep," he said, as if he was the one who had to justify my presence outside his room.

"I had that strange dream again," I said. "The dream about the African shaman."

Noah opened his door slightly wider.

"Want to come in?" he asked.

No, I just want to stand here in the corridor, chatting, I almost said. But I just nodded instead.

He let me in.

I chose to sit on the chair by his small desk, identical to the one I had just got up from in my own room, one floor up. I turned the chair toward the bed, where Noah sat, watching me silently.

"Can I talk to you about something without you thinking I am crazy?" I asked.

"I can't promise that," he said. "But you can try."

I sighed.

"How did you feel at the chateau in Chevy yesterday?" I asked. "What did you think when you saw the place, and the swords, and the painting...?"

105

"Strange," he said. "Very strange."

"Why do you think that is?" I asked.

"I am sure there is a perfectly logical explanation," he said.

"Such as?"

He shrugged.

"Just a coincidence."

"I understand what you mean…" I started slowly. "Except… except when I first met you again after all these years, when you nearly ran me over in the street…"

"You jumped in front of my car," he said. "And I stopped. That's something to my credit, I hope."

"You did," I said. "That's not the point…the point is…"

How am I going to get the point across to him? Where do I even start? With the seventeen-year-old Adele who wandered off to the nearby mountains on a spring day over two hundred years ago and got lost?

With the schoolteacher who saved her and accompanied her home, and then was too timid to ask for her hand in marriage?

Or with the choice this young woman made, under pressure, to marry a well-off merchant and have two children with him?

Or perhaps with how she left her husband and escaped to Paris, the city of her dreams, with the schoolteacher, leaving behind a broken family and broken hearts?

Or do I start with a story of an untimely death and of heartache? A story of heartbreak beyond imagination on the year of the French Revolution, the same year when a mob had stormed the Bastille but it was too late, too late for the French girl and her lover; her lover whose name he just saw the day before, amongst the display of swords in the Chateau de Chevry and perhaps recognized deep within him. The name of Jules Badeau, teacher and Master of Arms, who died old and lonely here, near Gex, in 1807?

I couldn't tell him any of that, for he surely would not understand.

"Yes, you're right," I said. "I am sure there's a perfectly logical explanation to all of this."

He slowly raised his hand and touched my cheek, then my lips, and then he pulled me toward him and kissed me.

TWENTY-SIX

Paris, 1789

A terrible hailstorm hit many parts of France and it was the topic of conversation everywhere that week. On top of the drought that lasted all spring, it was said that the recent hailstorm destroyed crops all over the country.

Adele sat in the front room with Monsieur Jacob and two guests, a man and a woman, when they heard a knock on the door. It was fierce, demanding.

Jules was away on business of a nature he did not wish to discuss with Adele, despite her having asked him several times, but Adele assured him she would be fine in the company of Madame and Monsieur Jacob, in his absence.

Jules kissed her before he left and said it was better if she didn't know the details.

Adele enjoyed keeping company with the elderly couple and their many guests, some of whom would come and go daily. They always had interesting conversations, from which Adele learned many new things. For example, she heard how the nobility of Paris, many of whom resided in large country homes most of the year, led extravagant lifestyles while the people of France were hungry for food. How the King and his Austrian wife, Queen Marie-Antoinette, allowed themselves to eat and drink in one day what a thousand people would consume in a week.

"It cannot go on like this," said the young man seated with them—he had arrived that morning from Lyon. "People are dissatisfied, and the situation is only getting worse. Taxes are high and the crops are not successful this year. There will be even less to go around. Something must be done."

"We all agree, citizen Charles," said Monsieur Jacob. "What we perhaps disagree on are the methods to be deployed."

"We cannot negotiate with them," said the young man with ardor. "Sadly, the only way to bring justice to the people is to take it by force."

"This is where I disagree," said the elegant woman. Her name was Marguerite, and according to Monsieur Jacob, she was a childless widow. About Adele's age, with dark hair and impressive green eyes, she sat upright in her seat and participated in the conversation as if it was obvious that her opinion was as important as that of Monsieur Jacob and the young man from Lyon.

Adele, after years of being pushed aside by a controlling husband, still did not feel at ease when such serious conversations were held and she was expected to contribute her opinion, but she was becoming more and more used to sitting in such meetings. When Jules was there, he would always ask her what she thought about this or that matter, and she loved him even more for this public display of appreciation.

Madame Jacob was out in town running some errands and Adele had just brewed a pot of coffee, noticing that the Jacob household was very low on sugar. *Perhaps they could not afford to buy more,* she thought. Times were hard for everyone in the summer of 1789. Many crops failed after the recent hailstorm and prices of grain skyrocketed. Coffee and sugar were a true luxury, which many could not afford, even in Paris. Adele hoped that at least her family back home, farming their own land, was spared some of the suffering.

They had been discussing the possible ways to help the *paysans*, the farmers who were having a difficult year with their crops being decimated due to the particularly harsh weather conditions.

"And due to the spending habits of the aristocracy," Marguerite said.

"People are hungry," said Monsieur Jacob. "While at Versailles they eat mutton and drink wine that has aged for fifteen years in their cellars, the people of France are starving."

"The queen walks around in silk and *indienne* dresses and eats cream cakes, while the people walk around in rags," said the young man. He still wore his travel clothes, and Adele didn't want to comment on the good quality of his own jacket and breeches, which were obviously not rags. She knew he was staying for the week with Monsieur and Madame Jacob in their guest room. He reminded her of Pierre Bertrand when he was young: the way he spoke; the very formed opinions that he considered more important than those of others around him; the expertly knotted cravat around his neck.

And then came the knock.

Monsieur Jacob raised a finger, signaling for the young man to go to another room. The man quietly disappeared as Monsieur Jacob approached the front door.

Three of the *Gardes Françaises,* the King's men, stood at the door, in their blue coats. Their red waistcoats looked ominous to Adele, as though they were bathed in the people's own blood. This was something she'd heard from one of the passing men the week before, and it had stayed in her mind.

"We are looking for a man, a suspect," said the tallest of the three.

Monsieur Jacob hesitated before answering.

"There are many men coming and going in this house," he finally answered. "I do not know who you are looking for."

The tall man looked at the other two, then at Monsieur Jacob.

"He is of average height and build, with dark hair," he then said. "He is an assassin."

Monsieur Jacob gasped.

"An assassin? Surely not in this house! My guests are all respectable men."

The tall man looked at his colleagues again.

"We have had reports," he said. "Someone reported him coming into this house."

"I can assure you..." started Monsieur Jacob.

"I am afraid you will have to accompany us, for questioning," the guard interrupted him. "You can explain your activities and gatherings to my commander. Apparently, you have many regular gatherings here in your home, monsieur."

"*Bien, Citoyen,*" said Monsieur Jacob. "I shall get my vest then and we can go and discuss the matter with your commander."

The tall guard then turned to the two women still sitting in the front room.

"You should all get your vests," he then said.

"What? Why?" asked Monsieur Jacob, a voice that was just a notch too loud. "What are they accused of?"

The tall man straightened his back, looking even taller than he already was.

"You are all accused of conspiring against the King of France, monsieur," he said.

Adele was lifted on horseback by strong arms—the horse itself was a black creature of immense beauty and she could not help but notice its dark, shiny coat; it felt so soft to the touch. She was sat sideways, in front of the tall officer, who led the group through the streets of Paris.

Monsieur Jacob was forced to walk alongside them, while the other woman—Adele could not remember her name now—rode in front of another of the King's Guards. They did not search well enough to find the young man hiding in one of the back rooms—they seemed content with the three people they were bringing in—and Adele could not stop thinking about the randomness of it all. What if she hadn't been in? What if Jules had been there with them?

Adele now wondered what the young man would do—could he help save them? Would he await Madame Jacob's return and report the events to her? And would the two of them work out a plan, call for help?

And Jules? Would he come for her? He was not due back for another week. He said that the less she knew, the better it would be for her. Now she understood what he meant.

As they rode along the cobbled street at a fast walking pace, Adele could feel her heart pounding. Where were they taking them? She looked down and saw Monsieur Jacob struggling to keep up. She turned to the officer sitting behind her on the horse.

"Monsieur, you are forcing an old man to walk faster than he is able!" she said in a quiet voice, hoping for the best.

The tall man didn't answer but slowed his horse.

"Where are you taking us?" asked Adele.

Again, he did not say anything.

The answer became clear a few moments later, as they crossed the bridge to the Île de la Cité and approached the Palais de le Cité and the Tour de l'Horloge, which, with its imposing tower, stood guard next to the Palais.

"Surely not the Conciergerie!" mumbled Adele.

The Conciergerie, which was part of the Palais, served as a prison, this much she knew. This is where many friends ended up, Jules told her on one of their evening strolls along the Seine.

"Never to be heard from again," he added.

"They put prisoners there for no reason, just because they speak for the people," said Jules to her that evening.

And now, were they really being taken there?

She tried to catch Monsieur Jacob's eye but the elderly man walked with his head down, still struggling to keep up. She could see he was short of breath.

The horses came to a halt outside an imposing gate, guarded by men with muskets. They were waved through into an internal courtyard, where they all dismounted. The tall guard was surprisingly gentle as he took Adele's hand and helped her off the back of the horse.

Despite her fear she looked around and upward, admiring

her surroundings. The rays of the afternoon sun bounced off the slates of the conical roofs above the turrets.

If only Jules were there with her, he'd know what to do. But Jules was far away, where exactly she did not know. And an ominous feeling, perhaps a premonition, made her wonder whether she would ever see him again.

Moreover, she wondered if she might ever see her family again—her children, her parents, even Pierre. Would she ever be able to explain what made her leave them behind and go to Paris with Jules? Would they ever understand? Would they forgive her? She had the feeling that now she might never find out.

TWENTY-SEVEN

Paris, 2018

After that, we went to Paris.

How we got there, I cannot explain. Because when we woke up just after midday, our naked bodies entangled like vines and the few bright summer rays sneaking through the drawn curtains and signaling it was perhaps time to get up, and when all the tears dried on our cheeks and the sweat on our bodies evaporated, we lay under the sheets together, not knowing where one of us began and the other ended, and I said: "Let's go to Paris. It might help me understand some things."

"Okay," he said, and that was it. There was no "why" or "how" or "if." The lack of words, the fact that there was no need to explain and to reason, the pure acceptance of what felt right was something I had never experienced before in my relationship with a man.

We packed our bags and left them at the hotel reception. We checked out and found a place nearby to have lunch, which was in fact breakfast, and went back to the hotel to get our bags and call a taxi to take us to the Cornavin train station, in the center of Geneva.

We sat together on the nearly three-hour train journey holding hands, but we did not speak. We could not speak. It was almost as if we were living one of my past-life regression experiences. Our silent train journey had a dreamlike quality to it, which neither of us wished to disturb.

I fell asleep with my head on Noah's shoulder and slept for an hour or so, a deep but tormented sleep. When I awoke, I had only fragments of dreams, or perhaps they were memories. I saw a distressed Frenchwoman, crying. An old man shuffling his feet, his head bowed in anguish, walking on a cobbled street while three horsemen rode next to him, taking him to prison.

I saw crowds shouting, calling out for a revolution. "Down with the aristocrats," they chanted. "Down with the King."

I saw Adele's terrified eyes, as she was being taken toward a beautiful, imposing stone building, its gray cone-shaped spires gleaming in the afternoon sunlight. Yet Adele, probably in her late thirties now, could hardly breathe. She was terrified, dreading the moment she got there. The feelings of sadness and fear were overwhelming.

Or perhaps it was I, Amelia, not Adele, who was feeling so terrified, so breathless, as I awoke next to Noah on the train speeding through the French countryside.

Perhaps it was I, Amelia, who was in fact Adele, or she was I—I did not know anymore. But how else could I explain the paralyzing sense of dread I felt as the train approached the Gare de Lyon, a place I'd been to several times before?

TWENTY-EIGHT

West Africa, 1577

He dug up the strange object from the ground, and then held it firmly in his hands. When he buried it some twenty moons ago it was shiny, it sparkled in the sunlight. Now, it was a strange dark color, as if the ground it was buried in made it rot. But it wasn't rot, just dirt, for when he scraped it with his fingernails, and then wiped it with a cloth, its shine started coming through again. This made the young man happy.

It was cool to the touch. He liked how it felt in his hands. It made him feel powerful, even if he could not tell exactly what were the magic powers this thing possessed.

He tried to imitate the gestures he'd seen in his dream, the stabbing and slashing motions. They made him feel energized, as if that same energy that flowed through him when he was healing also came to him when he was using this magical tool.

And then he sensed that someone was watching him, and he put the strange stick down.

He looked around him but could see no one. Was it the forefathers watching? Was it his mentor?

But no, a rustling of leaves not far from him, at the edge of the forest, indicated that someone was indeed there, a physical presence. He spotted some dark hair, a bit of smooth skin.

"Who's there?" he called out. "Show yourself."

A rustling of leaves again, a woman's laughter, and the sound of running feet.

He caught a glimpse of something, of someone running away—could it possibly be Mukambu? Was she hiding there, watching him play with the ghost-men's stick?

He held on to the pointed stick, hesitating whether to bury it in the ground again, and decided against it. If it did possess magical powers, they did not seem to work against him. Perhaps this is what the dream was all about—maybe the shaman was telling him to use this stick for strong magic? To help him become a warrior of a different kind, not the kind that sheds blood or maims others, but the kind of powerful warrior who possesses control of the magic that perhaps this stick represents? And if, and just if, Mukambu thought that his control of this magical weapon was amusing, or interesting, perhaps he can use it to draw her to him?

He continued practicing with the stick and discovered it not only entertained him, but also made him stronger physically and mentally, more focused on his healing, more accurate with his moves.

It became a habit: every afternoon he would take the magic stick out of his hut, clean it with large soft leaves until it shone, and would practice turning it, slashing with it, stabbing his imaginary opponents. These opponents were always the ghostmen, the pale-faced savages who killed his master, his teacher, the beloved shaman, and took away so many of the young men he grew up with.

Mukambu was often there, at the edge of the forest, watching him from a safe distance. He learned to recognize her footsteps, the low rumble of her laughter when he made some particularly funny move with the magical stick. She knew that he knew she was there. It was a game they played, a game that neither of them dared take further.

Until one day, Mukambu found the courage.

She stepped out of the clearing where she usually hid, and watched him with her large dark eyes. Then she took a few steps toward him.

"Can I try?" was all she asked.

He handed her the magic stick, and she held it in her hands, carefully examining the ornate handle, enjoying the sleekness and the beauty of it.

She then tried to imitate the maneuvers she had seen the young man do so many times: the slashing and stabbing, waving the magic stick here and there.

"Careful," he said. "You might hurt yourself."

"What's it to you?" she asked.

"Then I'd have to heal your wounds," he said.

She laughed, handed the stick back to him, and walked away without another word.

The next day, she came back, and brought him a small gift—a straw basket she had woven herself.

"My mother asked me to bring this to you," she said. "To thank you for healing my sister."

"That was many moons ago," he said.

Mukambu shrugged.

"Time means nothing," she then said.

"It is just an illusion," he agreed.

Again, she walked away without saying another word.

TWENTY-NINE

Paris, 1789

The last Adele saw of Monsieur Jacob was when she was dragged in one direction, he in the other. She was taken, together with the other woman, Marguerite, to a dark, dirty cell.

As the two women were escorted to their cell, Adele was struck by the contrast between the beautiful exterior, the sunny Parisian day, and the putrid underground dungeons she was pulled through with Marguerite.

The two women were led through a gated archway and down a flight of stairs. Adele held her skirts up, for the ground was wet under her feet. Marguerite grabbed her hand.

"*C'est horrible...*" she whispered

"We'll be fine," said Adele, but her voice echoed in her own ears and even she could tell it was trembling.

"Why are you locking us up here?" asked Adele softly, not wanting to hear her own voice breaking off the dark walls around her.

"Treason," said the guard. "Conspiring against our King, the honorable Louis the Sixteenth," he mumbled. "All of you down here, you are all traitors."

"But *Monsieur*," started Marguerite. "You know just as well as we do that everyone says the same thing: the people are hungry. This does not make us traitors, does it? You, too, have to feed your family."

The guard hesitated for a brief moment before locking the gate behind him. It seemed as if Marguerite's words found a listening ear, but it was not enough to get them out of the trouble they just found themselves in.

The *Gardes Françaises*, despite being very much part of the people, and witnessing the injustice everyone had to endure at the hands of the nobility, held their loyalty to the King above all.

"I will bring you food later," was all he said before he turned his back on them and left them locked in their cell. Adele thought, or maybe hoped, that she detected some kindness in his voice.

In the semi-darkness she could make out the outlines of two small beds, two large bedpans, nothing else.

They could hear the guard's steps echoing on the stone floor as he walked away and back up the stairs.

"What now?" asked Adele, and Marguerite sighed.

"We can only hope that our friends will soon find a way to get us out of here, somehow—I don't see myself surviving here more than a week."

"That guard," said Adele. "He listened to you, to what you had to say. Did you see that? He knows we are right. He knows we are not traitors."

"Everyone knows we are right," said Marguerite. "But it doesn't change anything, because until the people take the power into their own hands, they will be trampled upon by those who have the money, and the food, and no interest in relinquishing any of it."

Adele trembled.

"You are a widow," she said hesitantly. She'd just met Marguerite that very morning, and did not wish to ask her questions that would make her uncomfortable. But their present circumstances were beyond uncomfortable, and so she felt this would not matter so much anymore.

"Yes," said Marguerite. "My husband was in the service of a nobleman. We lived on his estate, and my husband was one of his servants, a faithful servant at that. He served him for many years, and I took care of the Master's children when they were young, I was their governess."

Adele waited for her to continue.

"I always tried to keep out of the Master's way, for he'd look at me most inappropriately. I wouldn't have minded if it were just looking, but he was a revolting man, and when he tried to touch me again and again, I told my husband."

Marguerite's voice was breaking now.

"Perhaps I shouldn't have said anything. I wouldn't have said anything, had I only known..."

She wiped a tear and Adele moved closer to her, held her hand.

"My husband was outraged, he wanted to confront the Master," she continued. "I tried to talk him out of it, but it only got worse. I could not do my work without the horrid man following me around. He even tried once when his children were in the same room! And so..."

She hesitated.

"And so, one day, my husband confronted him. He said he no longer wanted me to work as the governess of the children. The nobleman understood everything, and the following day had my husband arrested for thieving—he claimed he'd stolen money from his rooms, which of course was a complete lie."

She was now crying silently, and Adele hugged her.

"I am so sorry..." she said.

"He was taken away, and three days later, he was dead. They said it was an accident, but of course it was no accident...it was no accident. I took my few possessions and ran away from there, to the home of my sister and her family. They took me in. That was nearly eight years ago, so you see...injustice prevails and the corrupt and evil have the power. But this cannot continue, for the people of France will have to change it—and in the meantime, you and I need to try and save our skins, not to be left and forgotten in this horrid place."

Adele nodded silently.

THIRTY

Paris, 2018

The Paris I encountered that afternoon was nothing like the city I remembered from my previous visits. On my visit some months back, as well as on previous work visits some years back, Paris to me was just another wonderful, romantic tourist destination.

However, the Paris I walked into from the Gare de Lyon was another place altogether, one where I could easily imagine horses trotting on filthy streets, passing by children in rags, and pulling behind them carriages glistening in the sunlight. A Paris where arrogant noblemen rode on horseback while the poor groveled in their hunger and misery.

Something in me shifted, as if a dam had burst. I was suddenly able to let go of the daily worries that troubled me—my work, my children, my frustrating relationship with Don, and my developing relationship with Noah. Now, the bigger picture seemed elsewhere—not in my petty worries that seemed as if they were the most important things in the world just yesterday—but in a life that I may, or may not, have had some centuries back.

Because if this was possible—and I was still not convinced that I actually believed it was possible—then it changed everything.

Because if another lifetime as another person was something that could be real, then everything I've lived for and everything I believed in until now—who I am or the person I thought that I was—was something of an illusion.

I held tight to Noah's hand as we came out of the metro at Saint Germain.

After being turned away from two hotels—"Sorry *madame,* we are fully booked," was the answer from both of the places we tried—we checked in to a small hotel on one of the side streets, which happened to have one room available.

"You are very lucky, *Madame et Monsieur,*" said the soft-spoken woman at reception. "We just had a cancellation. You only need one room, correct?"

Noah looked at me as I nodded.

"Yes, please," I said. "We'll take the one room you've got. Thank you."

We left our bags in the room and went back into the Parisian afternoon sun, taking in the busy Quartier Saint Germain with its upmarket shops and sophisticated cafés. We were not walking anywhere in particular, we were more like two people floating in a daydream through familiar territory, although as Noah revealed when we arrived at the Gare de Lyon, this was his first visit to Paris.

"It's my first visit to France," he admitted.

Now he was taking in the sights and smells and seemed to be enjoying them.

"But it is strange how it seems familiar, in a way," he said. "I can't explain it. But don't ask me to believe all that weird past life stuff. I am not quite ready for that."

"I am not sure that I am," I admitted. "But since I met you I… don't know. Things are just getting weirder and weirder."

He looked at me and smiled, the first time I'd seen him smile in months. The smile brightened his face, made him look younger.

"I'll take it as a compliment," he said.

"It is, I guess," I said.

The exchange between us suddenly got lighter; tensions vanished. Now our legs carried us through small cobbled alleys to places we didn't know, but we did, we probably did know them on some level, for when we entered the small Rue de Buci Noah's fingers tightened around mine.

He stood still for a moment or two, as if taking in the narrow sidewalk and everything around him. He absorbed the laid-back atmosphere, the cafés filled with smartly dressed people. They all seemed relaxed, sitting on chairs outside, enjoying the early evening with glasses of wine in front of them. Olives and peanuts were served in small glass dishes on each table—the traditional aperitif before the late dinners on this summer day. It was the same on many other Parisian streets in July, but this was different, for Noah was almost shaking.

"I do know this place," he said.

He took my hand and turned the corner onto the Rue Grégoire de Tours, past a flower shop and a yellow storefront, with big black hand-painted letters over the entrance spelling, "Buci News." He led me to a red door to the left of Buci News, and then stood in front of it as if he was under some kind of spell.

"Here," he said. "Here."

"What's here?" I asked, for the place didn't look familiar to me. I had no idea what he was talking about.

"Here..." he said slowly. "I know this place."

"What do you mean?" I asked, trying to push the door open.

"Don't," he said, pulling my hand away from the door. "In any case, it's locked, you need a code to get in."

He pointed at the small keypad with letters and numbers to the right of the door. Like in many Parisian buildings, instead of a key, anyone wanting to enter the building needed to know the code.

"We can try inside here," I pointed to Buci News. "Let's talk to them, ask about this building."

Noah allowed me to drag him into the store but stood by the entrance like a statue. I could tell his dark mood was back.

"*Pardon*," I approached the young man behind the counter. "Excuse me, but my...my friend lived here many years ago, right next door. Do you know what's there now?"

The young man looked at me from behind his round, wire-framed glasses and smiled.

"Oh, Monsieur Clement, the owner of the store, lives there. Would you like to talk to him? He is out for the evening, but will be here tomorrow morning."

"Thank you," I said. "Thank you so much."

Noah still stood by the door, as if frozen in his spot.

"Come on, Noah," I said. "Let's find a nice place to have dinner. We'll come back tomorrow morning."

THIRTY-ONE

Paris, 1789

Adele did not know how many days and how many nights passed in that cell. It was as if they'd been forgotten, her and Marguerite. The meager rations of food—lukewarm broth and dry bread, were not enough to keep their bellies full, but they didn't feel hungry.

Marguerite cried day and night—she was used to relative comfort and could not get enough sleep on the hard mattress, covered by the itchy, foul-smelling blanket they were given. The pretty clothes she wore when she walked into the cell were now in urgent need of a wash; her beautiful dark hair hung in uncombed lumps. She was a shadow of her former self.

As for Adele, she did not care so much for the lack of comfort or lack of food. All she could think about was the lack of communication—with Jules, and also with her family.

When she left them in such haste nearly a couple of months before, she did not think ahead. She just assumed that in the future, somehow, everything would be all right. Now the future looked bleak. In fact, she was not certain there would be a future at all. Perhaps she would be left to rot in that cell, to die without anyone knowing where she was.

She felt certain Jules would do everything in his power to come for her, to help her, but what…what if he couldn't? What if he didn't know where she was, or what if something happened to him, something…something awful? What if he, too, was now locked up in some horrible cell, or worse—what if he was dead? Then she, too, would surely perish here because no one knew of her whereabouts. No one but Monsieur Jacob, who was taken to the Conciergerie at the same time as her and Marguerite. But he was old, frail, and perhaps he would not survive the experience.

Marguerite moaned in her sleep. Adele got up from her own uncomfortable bed and sat by Marguerite, stroking her hair.

"Shhh," she said. "Shhh, everything will be okay."

Marguerite seemed to have drifted back into deep sleep and Adele lay awake for what seemed like hours, until what appeared to be the sunrise. It was hard to tell in that underground cell, but there was the faintest change in the shade of darkness in the corridor outside their cell. She could hear some movement in the corridor—it wasn't footsteps—perhaps a scurrying rat? The thought terrified her and she covered her head with the thin, foul-smelling blanket.

What a long distance this was, she thought, from those wonderful meals with Madame and Monsieur Jacob just a week or so ago, from the evening walks along the Seine with Jules in the past weeks. This did not make any sense, why did she deserve this?

A sneaking suspicion came creeping, and she tried to push it out of her mind. Maybe she deserved this because...because... but no, she didn't believe in such things. If indeed there was a punishing God up there, one who saw all the bad deeds we did and made us suffer for them, He would surely have not held her choices against her. He would have understood that she had no real choice. Was she to regret her actions now, repent for them in order to escape this terrible destiny, this terrible misunderstanding?

THIRTY-TWO

Paris, 2018

The next morning I woke up late. I expected to find Noah next to me—where he was the previous night when I fell asleep—but he was not in the room. I could smell his scent on the pillow he'd slept on, and hugged it for a little while, taking in something that I could not put into words.

I showered and dressed, and since it was after nine and there was no sign of him, I sent him a text message and went down for breakfast.

I had my croissant, orange juice and coffee, and there was still no sign of Noah. How strange. Where could he be?

I decided not to waste the beautiful sunny Parisian morning.

"Can you please give this note to Monsieur Welder if he comes in? Mr. Noah Welder…he has dark hair and…"

"*Oui, oui*, the monsieur was here this morning, the American, correct? He said he went to the *salle d'escrime*…"

"*Salle d'escrime*? You mean the fencing salle?"

"*Oui, oui*, the fencing… what do you call it?"

The elderly lady waved an imaginary sword around.

"*Oui*, he asked me this morning if I know a salle d'escrime nearby. Of course, there are many in Paris but he wanted the old one…"

I was trying to make some sense of what this lady was trying to tell me.

"So do you know where he went? Did he leave a message?"

"No, no message," she said. "But maybe he went to this one here…"

She took out a map of the city and pointed at a small street not far from the river.

"*C'est la rue Gît-le-Cœur*, here in the 6th arrondissement," she said. "There is an old *salle d'armes*. I think he went to this one. It's only ten minutes to walk from here."

"Thank you," I said. "Thank you so much."

Why didn't he wait for me? Perhaps he wanted some time alone, to explore his memories, his feelings, his doubts? Maybe I shouldn't go looking for him?

First, I went back to Buci News, in hope I would find the owner, Monsieur Clement. Perhaps he could shed some light on what was upstairs, in the building above the store?

Monsieur Clement was indeed there, a kind gentleman in his sixties. He raised his head from the morning paper as I walked in.

"*Bonjour, madame*," he greeted me, and I smiled at him.

"*Bonjour*, are you Monsieur Clement?" I asked.

He nodded.

I hesitated for a short moment.

"The young man who was here yesterday afternoon, he said you might be able to help me...help us. My...my companion and I are visiting Paris. We are from New York. My companion, he is a fencing coach. He has gone to visit a fencing *salle* but he thinks that the building next door is very familiar to him. He thinks someone he knows lived there once, perhaps..."

My voice lingered as I was trying to explain this to Monsieur Clement, in a way that would not sound completely crazy.

"I've lived there for the past twenty years," said Monsieur Clement. "But it is a very old building, you know, over two-hundred years old. I bought the building—this store and the two apartments above—from a young man. He said that this building had been with his family for nearly two centuries, but he was leaving France, to live overseas. I paid him a nice sum for it, too. I am still paying the mortgage on it."

"Do you remember the young man's name?" I asked.

"Let me think," said Monsieur Clement, cleaning his glasses. "His name was…yes, it was Monsieur Jacob. Jacques Jacob, if I remember correctly."

"Thank you," I said. "Thank you so much."

I bought a notebook and a pen for I did not want to leave the store empty handed after Monsieur Clement had given me his time, as well as a piece of mind-numbing information. Monsieur Jacob. What were the chances that this was a coincidence? Was this Monsieur Jacob's house? Was the young man who sold the building his great-grandson? I made a quick note in my newly purchased notebook.

"Try to find out about Monsieur Jacob," I scribbled while standing on the sidewalk, in front of Buci News.

I then headed east, toward the river, along the Rue de Buci that was full of cafés and small stores.

I turned left on the Rue Saint-André des Arts and within a few minutes stood in front of another red door, which looked freshly painted. The black and gold sign above it, *Salle d'Armes*, left no doubt. This is where the lady had sent me—but where was Noah?

A small brass sign to the left of the door announced the opening hours—5–8:30 pm, daily. It was now just before 10 am.

As I turned to leave, the red door opened and Noah came out, almost knocking me off my feet. I held on to his arm to steady myself and he held on to me as if I was his lifeline to reality. His eyes were red.

"Is everything okay?" I asked. "What happened?"

He didn't answer but pulled me toward him for a long embrace.

Then he took my hand and led me toward a nearby café.

"I need time to digest all this," he finally said.

"What do you mean?" I asked and then regretted it. He obviously needed some space.

We sat at a corner table, and ordered two coffees. It was a strange feeling, which I also needed time to digest—my sitting with Noah at a Parisian café, far from our everyday lives, and yet so close.

I could not quite put my finger on the reason for the ups and downs we had together—why sometimes I felt as if he was the closest person to me on earth, and other times, as if he couldn't be farther away, on another planet. Was it his Aspergerian moods? Was it my decision to give Don another chance? Did Noah feel as if I'd betrayed him in some way?

At times we had so much to say to each other and now—now the silence was powerful, full of meaning. But I wasn't quite sure what the meaning of it was.

"I know I've been here before, it is all so familiar," he finally said.

"How did you get into the *salle*?" I asked. "The sign says it's only open in the evenings."

He sighed.

"If I told you, you wouldn't believe me," he said.

"Try me."

"I woke up early, you were still sleeping," he said. "I had this urge to go out and explore, as if something was calling me. So I got dressed and went downstairs and asked the woman at reception if she knew anything about fencing in Paris. I told her I was a fencing coach in New York. She told me how big fencing was in France and how their current Sports Minister was an Olympic épeeiste—I didn't know that. Then she said there were several fencing *salles* around but that the oldest one was on a small street just a few minutes' walk away. So I took the address from her and walked here, only to find the door locked. Normal, I guess, at seven thirty in the morning."

"So how did you get in?" I repeated my question.

"That's where it gets interesting," he said.

"As I was about to leave, this guy shows up with a fencing

bag, and starts unlocking the door. I said to him I was a fencing coach, and he invited me in for coffee—he had a private lesson with someone booked for eight, before the guy's work I guess, and so had only a short time before his student arrived."

"So you went in for a coffee, and to have a look around," I said. "And...?"

"It's the most amazing *salle* I've ever seen," he said. "Full of old memorabilia, old weapons, old posters, old masks. It is just stunning—felt like stepping back in time."

I waited for him to continue.

"So the guy makes coffee, has a quick chat with me in his really funny English, and then his student arrives. So he says I can stay and look around," he said.

"So I watch the lesson a bit to learn something about French techniques, wander around the *salle* and look at the old stuff. I just don't feel like getting out of there, it feels like being home in some strange way. I'm sorry, I knew you were probably going to wake up and look for me, but I just couldn't leave. I can't explain it."

"It's okay," I said. "I think I know what you mean."

"And then I look at an old foil," he said. "And there's this name engraved on it."

"What name?" I asked.

"That name, you know," he said. "That name."

"What name? Tell me."

"The same name we saw in the chateau in that small town. That French name. Jules something."

"Jules Badeau?" I asked in disbelief.

"Yes, that's it," he said. "Jules Badeau."

THIRTY-THREE

Paris, 1789

The next morning Marguerite could not get out of bed. She shivered under the thin blanket and mumbled words Adele could not understand. Adele took her own blanket and wrapped it around Marguerite's feet. They felt cold and Adele took each foot between her two hands and tried to warm it up.

That's when she noticed the rash—pin-sized red bumps that were visible even in the dark underground cell, through the faded rays of light.

"Marguerite, can you hear me?"

She tried to wake her friend but all she got in return was delirious mumble.

Adele got to her feet and started banging on the metal gate.

"*Monsieur*, please, come and help…"

It took a while before a guard unlocked the door, took one look at Marguerite, and called out, "*Encore une,* another one!"

"What do you mean?" asked Adele, trying to stop the tears.

"They are falling like flies," said the guard, "with this dreaded disease."

"Dreaded disease?" whispered Adele. "What should we do?"

"She won't last long," said the guard and slammed the gate behind him.

For the first time since she'd been put into the cell together with Marguerite—was it days? Was it weeks?—Adele broke down and wept. Her own sobs echoed and sent shivers up her spine.

She felt a hand on her arm.

"Don't cry, Adele…"

Marguerite's weak voice came from a long distance away.

"I'm sorry," said Adele, wiping her eyes with her sleeve. "I am so sorry, I didn't mean to…"

"Adele," whispered Marguerite, "Can I ask you something?"

"Sure, Marguerite, what is it?"

"My sister…" Marguerite whispered. "If you make it out of here, please tell her that I love her and that I am sorry…Sorry for everything…"

Her voice drifted.

"Stop it, Marguerite," Adele's voice was soft, but the dread in it was unmistakable. "You'll be all right, you will recover…"

"No, Adele," she whispered back. "I won't, I know it."

"What nonsense," said Adele as she put her hand on Marguerite's hot forehead. "The doctor will come soon and will give you some medicine and you will…"

They both knew she was not telling the truth.

Marguerite sighed quietly and closed her eyes.

THIRTY-FOUR

Paris, 2018

We decided to walk toward the Hotel de Ville.

"It's beautiful," I told Noah. "It's such a fantastic building, one of the prettiest I've ever seen."

He just nodded, as if he didn't care which way we headed. We held hands, or to be truthful, Noah held on to my hand, as if he would be lost without it.

I led us toward the Pont Saint-Michel on the Rue Danton, and as we crossed the bridge the water of the Seine under our feet sparkled in the sunlight.

Then something made me freeze. My legs would not move, would not let me walk on the Boulevard du Palais toward the Pont au Change to get to the other side of the Seine.

"What is it?" asked Noah. I could only point.

To our left stood a large, old building.

"It's the courthouse," said Noah, reading his map. "*Palais de Justice*, right?"

His voice sounded strangely French, his pronunciation was perfect.

"Not that," I shook my head. "Look."

To the right of the courthouse stood the Tour de l'Horloge du palais de la Cité, an ornate tower-clock nearly hidden by trees. But it was not the tower-clock that took my breath away and made the blood drain from my face—it was the building right underneath it.

"What is it, Amelia?" asked Noah, his voice not much more than a whisper. He felt it too, I was sure of it, but could probably not find the words, just like me.

We stood there for a few moments, holding hands in silence, trying to make sense of what we were feeling, what we were experiencing.

And we could still not find words to describe it to each other. For me, it was a feeling of dread; it was a premonition. A premonition that something very wrong was going to happen— or perhaps already happened? Could it have already happened, right here, over two hundred years ago?

THIRTY-FIVE

Paris, 1789

After they took Marguerite's body for burial, the days became unbearable; the nights even more so.

Adele lay awake for hours, alone in that cell, her only company being the scurrying rats. There were other prisoners in cells nearby, but she couldn't see them, though, she would often hear them moan at night.

She completely lost her appetite. She almost lost the will to live, but she did retain a flicker of hope.

"What is the date, please?" she tried again when a different prison guard shoved a bowl of broth at her one afternoon.

"July 12," said the new guard. Although abrupt, at least he answered. She ate a small amount of the thin broth and stale bread he had brought in.

To keep her mind busy, Adele calculated—in thirteen days, on July 25, she would be turning thirty-eight. If she made it through the next two weeks, surely Jules would remember and come for her by then?

Her mind wandered back to her eighteenth birthday party, all those years ago, when Jules came to the party that her mother organized for her together with their neighbor—Madame Montague—in 1769. Twenty years, and they passed so quickly.

She laid on her low, narrow bunk, covered herself with the one blanket she had—for Marguerite's one was burned, for fear of spreading whatever disease she died of—and let her memory, or perhaps it was her imagination, transport her back to that warm evening in July, outside Madame Montague's barn.

In her fancy, she was wearing again the mustard-yellow dress her mother worked so hard to sew for her birthday party. She remembered the sleek fabric and the exact color of the dress, a yellow that was like the color of the setting sun over the fields in the Pays de Gex. She could almost touch the layers of lace around the collar and the hem. It was such a festive dress, and her mother worked so hard on it, only to be disappointed by her daughter who would run away to Paris twenty years later…to Paris, not with the man she had married, the one who promised he would take her there. But with the man she should have married, and didn't because she did not believe he could give her the kind of life she wanted.

She tried to push these thoughts to the back of her mind and concentrate on the memories, on the warm evening air, on how Jules Badeau showed up with a gift for her—a small rectangular locket on a beautiful gold chain. A locket that had her date of birth engraved on it in delicate, curly lettering—July 25, 1751. The locket that she had to return to Jules when she decided to marry Pierre. She wondered what became of that locket—did he melt it down and sell the gold? Did he keep it? What a silly idea. Why would he keep a locket with the date of birth of a girl who had married someone else?

Adele pushed that thought from her mind, too. She started shivering—she felt so cold all of a sudden—had she also contracted that dreaded disease, from Marguerite perhaps? But she didn't mind, she didn't much care whether she lived or died now. She just wanted to try and remember the food, the fantastic, festive food—and drink—her mother and the other village women helped prepare. Everyone loved a good feast and her eighteenth birthday was a wonderful excuse for a party, especially as her parents seemed keen to marry her off. The two obvious candidates were Pierre Bertrand, the well-off shop owner's son, and Jules Badeau, the schoolteacher who found her wandering in the mountains a few months earlier, when she took off in a storm of emotions and anger at her family. Jules helped her find her way home and visited her every weekend until...until the decision was made that she would marry Pierre.

But at that party, her eighteenth birthday, it was not yet clear how the cards would fall. She still had the possibility—as much as it would have disappointed her parents—to choose the schoolteacher, except he had never officially asked for her hand. Neither did Pierre Bertrand—not really—for it was all agreed between their parents. A modest dowry was arranged, although she knew for certain that Madame Bertrand, Pierre's mother, would have never agreed that her precious son would marry a *paysan*'s daughter had Pierre not insisted. Her father was a hardworking man—but true, he was a peasant—even her mother admitted to it, and to how the choice of marrying a man working the land had affected her, a respectable bookbinder's daughter. And so, in the end, the wedding was arranged by Pierre's meddling mother, and her family was given instructions that they should only invite a certain number of guests. After all, it was the groom's family who paid for the wedding.

Adele's delirious mind went back to that party—the party before life-changing decisions were taken. At that party she had danced with Pierre Bertrand, wearing her beautiful new dress, while Jules Badeau watched from afar, and did not ask her to dance. Why did he not ask her to dance?

She would probably never find out now; it was too late. Too late, too late, too late to apologize to Jules for marrying Pierre, to Pierre for leaving him for Jules, to her mother and her father for leaving them at their old age and to her children for going away while they were still young.

As for herself, she thought that she had had a good life, and even if she did not make it to her thirty-eighth birthday—she had a husband and children and love and even a trip to Paris. She was now here in the Paris that she so wanted to see, to explore, to live in—this same Paris but locked in a cell underground. Maybe she was forgotten, maybe abandoned. But surely, surely if Jules did not come for her it was because he couldn't. Perhaps he, too, was dead…dead like Marguerite, dead like the many who wanted to fight for a better future for France and for its people and to do away with the aristocracy and royalty who were bleeding their beloved country dry.

Her thoughts stopped making sense, even in her own confused mind, and she thought, perhaps imagined, that she could see Jules in the distance, opening his arms to her. And she ran, ran, ran toward him.

When she reached him, she noticed that in his hands he held something soft, with hues of gray and blue, and with awe Adele realized he was holding the fabric that she found on her doorstep all those years ago, the blue-gray silk she coveted when she went with her mother to the Bertrand store to choose material to make into a dress for Adele's eighteenth birthday party.

She had thought that the expensive fabric was a gift from Pierre Bertrand, she could not imagine that the schoolteacher, leading a modest life, could afford to gift her such a luxury. But he did, he did—she only found out after her wedding that it was not the man she married, Pierre Bertrand, who left the beautiful fabric for her, but the man she should have married, who had little but was willing to give her everything.

But why was Jules bringing her the fabric now? And how could he, as it was already made into a dress all this time ago, twenty years ago, was it not?

She let her consciousness slip into the darkness, the abyss.

THIRTY-SIX

West Africa, 1577

It was a lonely existence in that hut on the outskirts of the village. That much he already knew from watching his teacher, his mentor, over the many years of his apprenticeship. The old man had no family of his own, just like he—now a not-so-young man—had no one except for his mother. But he was not sure he would like to end his days like the shaman, an old man dying alone by the stump of a baobab tree in the center of the village.

And so, when his mother mentioned again that he needed a wife, he did not argue.

"I agree," he said instead. His mother read his lips, but she was not sure she understood correctly.

Again, she communicated her thought that he needed a wife with exaggerated hand gestures and grunts that made him smile.

I will not always be here to look after you, was what she tried to say. He understood.

"Yes, Mama," he said and hugged her. "I agree, I need a wife, and I know who she is—if she'll have me."

His mother gaped at him, wiping a tear from the corner of her eye.

The marriage was celebrated on a night with a full moon, as the couple danced to the drumbeat of the elders. The other villagers joined them in celebration—but there were mostly women, children, and some older men. All the young men were gone, and it was hard not to notice their absence, not to let it weigh down on the celebration that was subdued and much quieter than it would have normally been. Many of the burned huts were not restored. With fewer strong hands to rebuild them, there they stood, like charred, ghostly reminders to the atrocities the pale-faced men had committed not so many moons ago.

The young couple had settled into their married life—Mukambu moved into the shaman's hut and was proud to be the wife of the village witch-doctor. And the witch-doctor—he never forgot his mentor. He continued to converse with him in the dream world, and when he took the special herbs that helped him fly far away and meet with the old shaman, he always asked the same question. But it remained unanswered.

"What is the power of this magical stick?" he always asked. "What is its purpose?"

In his dreams, or herb-induced hallucinations, on the vivid journeys of his soul to consult with that of the old witch-doctor, he always carried that stick with him, for he knew it gave him special powers. It helped him fly.

The old man's staff was always with him, as well, inside the hut. It carried memories and the energies of the old shaman. But that sleek, shiny object, with the elaborate handle and the powerful sway, was the young shaman's prized possession, and he always kept it nearby. He even slept with it near him, despite Mukambu's complaints.

"One day," he told her, "one day, the ghost-men might come back to claim their magical stick, but it is mine now. It is mine now, and it will help me destroy them. I will destroy them with their own magic, with the weapon they left behind when they ran like cowards with the village's young men in chains. And so, until the day I die, I will always keep this magical weapon near me."

Mukambu didn't say anything, for she knew he was right, and that the pale-faced men would return one day. And on that day, she hoped the magical weapon would protect them all from the cruel ghost-men.

More from this author

Premonitions is Daniela's second novel. Her debut, *Recognitions*, was published by Roundfire Books in 2016 and the third book in this trilogy, *Precognitions*, is due out in 2020.

Daniela's other books, *On Dragonfly Wings: a skeptic's journey to mediumship* and *Collecting Feathers: tales from the Other Side* were published in 2014 and are available to order from your favorite bookshop and online.

Acknowledgements

The journey of *Premonitions*, my second novel, was quite different from that of *Recognitions*, the first in this trilogy.

Characters seemed to have taken on a life of their own and often manifested themselves in real-life people, only to disappear again, and wait for me on the pages of this book to allow them to do as they pleased.

And do as they pleased they did—taking me into their worlds, their memories, their problems, and their resolutions.

There are many real-life people who supported me on my writing journey, which alternated between France and the UK.

Jon Salfield, Maitre d'Armes extraordinaire and Head Coach at Truro Fencing Club helped with fencing-related advice and with editing the manuscript. In parallel to the publication of this novel, we co-authored a guide for fencers' parents titled: *From Last to First* (Liberalis, 2019).

Miroslav Lesichkov, head instructor and founder of the School of Medieval Swordsmanship MOTUS in Bulgaria, was my long-distance adviser on ancient swords.

Stephanie Roma King and Lior Bar-On, my beta readers, had advice and comments that were instrumental to the completion of this novel.

Friends and fellow writers at the Geneva Writers' Group and the founder Susan Tiberghien—author, poet, teacher, and ally—always provided encouragement, even when I was far away.

The wonderful team at John Hunt Publishing—my editor Mary Duffy and publishing director Dominic James, publicist Tracy Stewart, as well as Trevor Greenfield, Maria Barry, Beccy Conway, Mary Flatt, Stuart Davies, Nick Welch, and, of course—the inspiring John Hunt! You are all a real pleasure to work with.

And last, but not least—my family—the R team and the A team— who constantly put up with my writerly eccentricities and understand that when my characters speak, I am obliged to listen.

Daniela I. Norris
Truro, May 2018

About the Author

Premonitions is Daniela's second novel. She is a former diplomat and political writer turned inspirational author and speaker. Daniela lost her twenty-year-old brother in a drowning accident in May 2010. That was when she embarked on a journey of learning and exploration and her writing shifted from political to spiritual and inspirational. Daniela is the author of four books of non-fiction and short stories, and her first novel, *Recognitions*, was published in 2016. She lives with her family near Geneva, Switzerland, where she is working on the third novel in the *Recognitions* series, titled *Precognitions*, due out in 2020.

Daniela gives workshops and retreats on the themes of life plans, past lives, loss and grief, and is part of the International Grief Council—more details about her work and upcoming events on www.internationalgriefcouncil.org.

Website: www.danielanorris.com
Facebook: www.facebook.com/DanielaINorris/
Twitter: https://twitter.com/DanielaINorris

If you enjoyed *Premonitions*, please recommend the book to a friend and review it online.

Q&A with Daniela I. Norris

The characters in *Recognitions* and *Premonitions* are intertwined although they live in different eras and are of different ages and backgrounds. Did you find it difficult to connect between them?

I found that the connection between the characters of Amelia, a modern-day editor from New York, and Adele, a young woman from eighteenth-century France, came quite naturally. In fact, I first wrote the story of Adele, then the shaman, then the story of Amelia. After the three threads were written, it was like braiding a plait.

How is the shaman connected to Adele and Amelia?

This is a very good question and a great discussion point: one I am still in the process of answering myself as I am now writing the sequel to *Recognitions*, and *Premonitions,* titled *Precognitions.*

The shaman's character was there all along, and he is very important in both the lives of Adele, and of Amelia. He is like a shadow following them from one life to another. He is an important part of who they are and who they will become.

Can you say more about the sequel?

It is hard to talk about something that is still in the making; it's like a daydream unfolding in my mind. But I do plan a trilogy, with *Recognitions* being the first, *Premonitions* the second and *Precognitions* the third. *Precognitions,* due out in 2020, will have Jen, Amelia's daughter, as one of the main characters. Her relationship with her coach, Noah, is one of an apprentice-mentor, and transcends lifetimes.

The characters in *Recognitions* and *Premonitions* seem to have specific roles in each other's lives, do you think that people really have predetermined roles in other people's lives?

I don't know if people have predetermined roles in others' lives, but I always believed that some people act as 'flags' in the lives of others. Someone, often a stranger, can get us to do something or help us avoid doing something as if by chance - and then disappear from our lives. I believe it could be because their role in our lives was specific, punctual. Of course, there are others who might have much larger, more dominant roles in our lives. Others yet will accompany us on longer stretches of our lives' journeys.

You are a former diplomat, how does this affect your writing?

Many people wonder how someone who was into politics and international affairs for many years can turn to spiritual or inspirational writing – for me it is quite obvious. Politics keep us grounded, living in the here and now. Spiritual or inspirational writings can uplift us; can help us make this world a better place. One without the other would be difficult for many people, as not many of us can live in a spiritual bubble or in a monastery at the top of the world. Most of us need to live in the real world, and trying to see the 'bigger picture' through spirituality while keeping a tab on world events is, in my opinion, a healthy combination.

What are the themes of this trilogy?

I try to write about the themes of past lives in an interesting and grounded way. I don't see myself as a 'new age' writer, I see myself as a writer who is interested in many things, and my books are just a reflection of these interests. The themes of this trilogy are the (possibly) pre-determined roles of people we meet in our lives, reincarnation, past lives and the empowerment of young women.

How can readers learn more about theories of past lives or even life-between-lives?

There are many good researchers and writers out there who have published some fantastic books in the last thirty years or so. Namely – Dr. Brian Weiss, Dr. Michael Newton, Andy Tomlinson, Michael E. Tymn, David Fontana, Stafford Betty and many others. Their books are certainly worth reading if you want to learn more about these concepts. Different religions such as Buddhism, Hinduism and the Druze (an ethno-religious esoteric group) also have some fascinating writings and theories about those topics. These could be a great starting point.

Anything else you'd like to share with your readers?

It feels like I've shared a lot of my beliefs in *Recognitions, Premonitions* and in this Q&A session. I just want readers to know that I never try to convince anyone of anything. You don't have to believe in past lives to enjoy a good story, which is hopefully what I managed to achieve in this trilogy.

I don't want readers to feel as if spirituality or the topic of past lives are being imposed on them – they are merely offered as one possible explanation to experiences many of us have in our lives.

Lastly, please take a few moments to leave a review online, on the website of your choice. Reviews really help authors. It doesn't have to be long or gushing, it can be just one or two honest sentences. They will be much appreciated.

What readers are saying about *Recognitions*

This is a fascinating story exploring other areas of consciousness from reincarnation to far memory. It is also a gentle love story where all the threads are brought together. Living in New York, our heroine, Amelia, has reached an exceedingly stressful stage in her life, coping with divorce, two teenagers and an excessive workload to keep her head above water. Simultaneously she is trying to complete a long-unfinished novel. A friend suggests hypnotherapy, to help at least with sleeplessness.

Tentatively Amelia ventures for therapy. The counting down method for deep relaxation used by her therapist, Tatiana, takes Amelia into a form of regression. She slips back beyond her current life into a possible past life. She meets a young eighteenth-century teenager on a different continent

Adele is on the verge of womanhood, choosing her future. Leaving the therapist Amelia feels different, more alive, with enhanced awareness, being conscious of synchronicities. Strangely, she encounters a man from her past. The sudden awakening of these dormant memories overcomes Amelia's writer's block and she uses these characters to progress her novel with great excitement. Meantime, she still has to contend with her teenagers and ex-husband.

Having benefited, she has another session with Tatiana expecting more of Adele, but this time the imagery is of an ancient shaman. Thus, we have three differing stories running concurrently, woven into a fascinating braid culminating in a climax showing how deeply we are all a part of our roots

An intriguing read—our author knows her subject.

Valerie Dunmore, Society of Women Writers and Journalists

Recognitions by Daniela I. Norris centers on Amelia, who, under hypnosis and in dreams, sometimes encounters an intelligent French girl on the verge of choosing a future husband and sometimes an African shaman trying to save his village from sickness and slavery. As she struggles to understand her connection to these two people, her everyday relationships carry on with an ex-husband and two teenage children. When a man from her past comes into the picture and introduces her to fencing, the connections begin to click. I say "begin," because this first book of a trilogy leaves many questions open.

I have a sense that whatever any reader thinks is going on with past lives or collective consciousness, or the "something" the characters wonder about in Recognitions, the full story of the trilogy is going to turn out rather differently than predicted—but without the need for gimmicky plot twists. It is just that interesting, plus the tale is unfolding in the hands of a capable story-teller, which is clear from the very first chapter. Daniela I. Norris writes in clean, sparse prose, so she is able to paint the picture of three lives on three different continents with distinct voices for each without ever resorting to gratuitous description. As a result, the book moves at a fast pace, but without feeling rushed or empty. And even though I wanted to know how it would play out, I didn't skip a single word because every word was relevant in this engaging story.

— Readers' Favorite

Think *Cloud Atlas*, a classic story of rebirth, many lives, and reincarnation on a level that involves protagonists in other lives—but take it a step further in *Recognitions*, the first novel in a trilogy, which presents a woman under hypnosis who sometimes encounters a French girl on the cusp of marriage and sometimes an African shaman facing a village's struggles with illness and slavery.

Then take these diverse lives and weave them together in

the story of a modern-day woman, Amelia (who must deal with these other lives and her own daily challenges, and who faces her own struggle to understand the connections and messages that lie in her dreams and hypnotic state), and you have an emotionally charged saga filled with three threads that lead back to one tapestry of wonder.

Under a different hand, this saga of birth, death, and afterlife could have easily proved confusing: it's no simple matter to create three disparate, very different lives, and weave them together with purpose and discovery; no easy venture to bring all these pieces to life and then meld them into one.

It's also satisfying to note that the protagonist doesn't just skip into acceptance of these threads and their impact on her life; she's pulled in reluctantly and initially believes these results from hypnotherapy and dream states to be 'craziness'. She's no new age believer: she's a wife, mother, and has a life of her own: "I hardly have time to explore all sorts of strange mind-body-spirit connections or whatever they call them these days."

But it's a life destined to transform (though her husband's departure has already started the process of vast changes) in unexpected ways, and the gift here lies in how past, present, and future worlds not only connect, but collide.

There are many passages that support all kinds of emotional connections and disconnects, as well: "But I resolved to call Don later and tell him that there's something going on with our daughter. I'll call him even if talking to him will make me feel emotional, anxious, and envious of the quick fix he'd found in his life. Even if it would make me feel betrayed and confused by my feelings toward him—how his cynicism annoyed me for years, how I couldn't stand his macho jokes anymore and how relieved I had first felt when we decided to separate. We said we'd remain friends, for the kids' sakes. We said we'd see how it would go if we just parted amicably for a while, and then take it from there."

As Amelia's life changes and as her novel-writing is spiced by her dream states, she finds the courage to not only probe these events, but understand and incorporate them into her own world: "I needed to visit this place. This would help me understand more about Adele's world, it would be research, not some craziness destined to satisfy my sudden and illogical fascination with past lives, I said to myself." The result (much like Cloud Atlas's ability to make readers think far past the last page) is a story that is quietly compelling: a moving saga highly recommended for any reader interested in predetermination, past lives, and how three disparate worlds weave together.

—**D. Donovan**, senior reviewer, Midwest Book Review

The first book of Daniela Norris which I had read was *Collecting Feathers: Tales from The Other Side*. The book totally took me in a storm and changed my view of "The Other Side." *Recognitions* is the first novel by the author.

Recognitions is a book written in first-person narration by Amelia Rothman. But the story soon bifurcates into two other main characters, Adele Durant and an African Shaman, as the characters emerging from Amelia's hypnotherapy. The story swings between the three characters, initially with no relevance. But gradually, as the story unfolds, each of the character shows their relevance and brings out the complete picture.

The concept of the story is more of self-enlightenment and self-actualization. It plays around the concept of "Things that are meant to be." The writing style is simple and elegant. Daniela ensures that the reader is at pace with her narration and has no difficulty imagining the situations playing in the book. The descriptions of people and places are given in enough detail to create a picture but not that it feels dragged.

The characters vary their complexity depending upon the situations they are placed in. The characters, although are from different eras, blend well with each other throughout the story and bring out the best in the theme.

By the end of the book, a feeling of being enveloped by hope takes over. *Recognitions* is a book I shall definitely recommend everyone to read. It has a smooth flow and simple positivity to it. The upcoming parts in the trilogy definitely have something to catch up to, as this one surely has set a benchmark.

— **Devi Nair**, www.yogitimes.com

Whoa. This was a blast to read. *Recognitions* by Daniela I. Norris was incomparable to anything I have read in recent years. I do want to say though, that I don't think the cover does it one bit of justice at all. Definitely try not to judge this book by its cover, because it is so much more than what it appears.

A woman named Amelia suffers from anxiety after her husband up and leaves her. First of all, I could totally understand what this woman was going through, as I suffer from anxiety myself. One of the things that she said in the book really hit home with me. As Amelia is on her way to meet a hypnotherapist, she says that she doesn't know if she wants to get rid of her anxieties as they have sort of become part of her. This struck a chord with me, I have said that to my husband many times, so it was nice to see someone else who felt the same way as myself.

Amelia ends up going to the hypnotherapist anyway, and when she is put under hypnosis she has a vivid recollection of a girl named Adele, who is from France. This is just the beginning of many dreams and writings that she starts to experience revolving around this girl Adele.

Not only that, but there are things happening to her in her daily life that start to make her wonder if this is all connected, beginning with the return of someone from high school that she hadn't seen in 20 years. She wasn't ever really close to him, so she starts to wonder what he has to do with all of the things going on. Then everything just seems to connect from past to present, and in between. This was a stunning portrayal of past lives, interwoven and connected people, and learning to understand ones subconscious.

I don't think I have heard of many books like this that involved an adult main character, so that was really refreshing to see. This was a mixture of psychology (which I am going to school for), and a little bit of history, fantasy, and religious undertones all rolled into one great book. This book really came to life for me, and for that I give it 5 out of 5 stars.

— **Comfy Reading Blog,** https://comfyreading.wordpress. com/2016/02/26/recognitions/

Amelia is struggling with separation from her husband of [many] years, two teenage children, her job, and a novel that she has been writing. She agrees to hypnotherapy, although she has doubts about it.

What follows are creative inspirations, striking dreams, and surprising discoveries.

Recognitions is not one story. It is three different plots, each a treat in its own right.

As the author moves from one story to another, and then comes back, I, as a reader, was eager to find out how each one would pan out. And obviously, how the three will intertwine.

Adele, a French girl at crossroads in life. Does she make the right decision finally?

An African Shaman makes some tough choices.

Amelia is a witness to it all, initially wary. As she accepts changes in her old relationships, and paves a way for new, the three different tales merge.

Daniela I. Norris has weaved an emotionally potent tale that spans centuries and is connected through it all. Feelings don't change as generations do, do they?

The language is detailed, almost leisurely so, and yet, doesn't come across as unnecessarily verbose. It lingers on emotions, and thoughts, and events. Yet, it is engaging.

Recognitions ends with a certain contentment. A peace, that is satisfying.

Recognitions also leaves you with a need to know what comes next.

—Fascinating Quest Blog, http://www.nimiarora.com/

In general a great book. I had a long two-hour one-way drive to take—in order to help one of my sons fix his tractor. So, I logged onto Audible and did a real quick search and decided on *Recognitions* because of the sword on the front cover. I was thinking this was going to have lots of sword fights and generally gobs of blood and guts. Instead, what I got was a really captivating story about how our past lives affect our current ones. In fact, I was surprised that such a sensitive book captivated my attention.

Years ago, when I was in the Navy (stationed in the Far East) I was really into: transcendental meditation; personal mantras, spirit projection, out-of-body experiences, etc., etc. So, I was really engrossed by the book. In fact, it passed my "got to take a bathroom break as fast as I can" test.

The book itself was very disjointed. Jumping from current day New York, to 1700's France, to 1600's Africa. You would expect that a recording of such a book would be at least difficult to follow, But, the narrator did a superb job at switching meters, tones, and accents to give cue's as to where we were at. I really enjoyed listening to her quickly establish a place and time by: how formal she spoke, meters and tones she used, etc. She must have lots of experience doing this, but I could find another book that she had narrated??

To me, it seemed like a 'chick-book': lots of emotion, life issues, and extremely limited blood and guts (but, the crocodile scene made me squirm in my seat...kind of cool). So, it was not what I expected. Further, I would have not chosen it if I knew what it was about. But, still I really enjoyed it. Bravo. Next time

I take a long trip, I'll look for either this author or narrator. So, maybe...Just maybe...this was meant to be.
— **By manlystanley** on amazon.com

FICTION

Put simply, we publish great stories. Whether it's literary or popular, a gentle tale or a pulsating thriller, the connecting theme in all Roundfire fiction titles is that once you pick them up you won't want to put them down.
If you have enjoyed this book, why not tell other readers by posting a review on your preferred book site.

Recent bestsellers from Roundfire are:

The Bookseller's Sonnets
Andi Rosenthal
The Bookseller's Sonnets intertwines three love stories with a tale of religious identity and mystery spanning five hundred years and three countries.
Paperback: 978-1-84694-342-3 ebook: 978-184694-626-4

Birds of the Nile
An Egyptian Adventure
N.E. David
Ex-diplomat Michael Blake wanted a quiet birding trip up the Nile – he wasn't expecting a revolution.
Paperback: 978-1-78279-158-4 ebook: 978-1-78279-157-7

Blood Profit$
The Lithium Conspiracy
J. Victor Tomaszek, James N. Patrick, Sr.
The blood of the many for the profits of the few . *Blood Profit$* will take you into the cigar-smoke-filled room where American policy and laws are really made.
Paperback: 978-1-78279-483-7 ebook: 978-1-78279-277-2

The Burden

A Family Saga

N.E. David

Frank will do anything to keep his mother and father apart. But he's carrying baggage – and it might just weigh him down ...

Paperback: 978-1-78279-936-8 ebook: 978-1-78279-937-5

The Cause

Roderick Vincent

The second American Revolution will be a fire lit from an internal spark.

Paperback: 978-1-78279-763-0 ebook: 978-1-78279-762-3

Don't Drink and Fly

The Story of Bernice O'Hanlon: Part One

Cathie Devitt

Bernice is a witch living in Glasgow. She loses her way in her life and wanders off the beaten track looking for the garden of enlightenment.

Paperback: 978-1-78279-016-7 ebook: 978-1-78279-015-0

Gag

Melissa Unger

One rainy afternoon in a Brooklyn diner, Peter Howland punctures an egg with his fork. Repulsed, Peter pushes the plate away and never eats again.

Paperback: 978-1-78279-564-3 ebook: 978-1-78279-563-6

The Master Yeshua

The Undiscovered Gospel of Joseph

Joyce Luck

Jesus is not who you think he is. The year is 75 CE. Joseph ben Jude is frail and ailing, but he has a prophecy to fulfil ...

Paperback: 978-1-78279-974-0 ebook: 978-1-78279-975-7

On the Far Side, There's a Boy
Paula Coston
Martine Haslett, a thirty-something 1980s woman, plays hard on the fringes of the London drag club scene until one night which prompts her to sign up to a charity. She writes to a young Sri Lankan boy, with consequences far and long.
Paperback: 978-1-78279-574-2 ebook: 978-1-78279-573-5

Tuareg
Alberto Vazquez-Figueroa
With over 5 million copies sold worldwide, *Tuareg* is a classic adventure story from best-selling author Alberto Vazquez-Figueroa, about honour, revenge and a clash of cultures.
Paperback: 978-1-84694-192-4

Readers of ebooks can buy or view any of these bestsellers by clicking on the live link in the title. Most titles are published in paperback and as an ebook. Paperbacks are available in traditional bookshops. Both print and ebook formats are available online.

Find more titles and sign up to our readers' newsletter at
http://www.johnhuntpublishing.com/fiction

Follow us on Facebook at https://www.facebook.com/JHPfiction
and Twitter at https://twitter.com/JHPFiction

Printed and bound by PG in the USA